Cozy Therapy Dog - Connecting the Dots

A Truman Blue Mystery
Book 1

A story by Jane McAllen

(If you find typos, it is because Truman Blue was trying to get the author's attention by flipping her arm off the keyboard or mouse.)

Dedicated to those who assisted me in birthing this series

It took a village.

Linda Motes

Caroline Gausline

Stacey Stokes

And especially

Margie Vlasits

Jeanine Underwood

Carolyn Kidder

Barbara Kidder

And my sister Susan Connell who, before colon cancer extinguished her life, encouraged me to tell my stories.

The format of this book is set up with less than traditional white space to conserve paper.

To learn more about the real life Truman Blue, visit www.trumanbluemysteries.com

This book is a work of fiction. Except for Truman Blue who is a real therapy dog, names, characters, places and events are creations of the author's imagination, or fictionally represented. Any resemblance to actual people, events, or locations is completely coincidental.

All copyright laws apply. Revised September 2021.

Opaque curtains arrested the afternoon light. One woman pretended to sleep. One woman lay silent. A figure turned from the silent woman and left the room.

Chapter 1

"She's dead, you know?" Anna's age-worn voice cracked like an old porch rocker on ancient wooden planks. Her eyes flickered in accusatory slits.

"Meredith?" I asked.

Anna nodded. Her hand twitched on the arm of her wheelchair.

Why was Anna looking at me and my trainee Judith as if her roommate's death were our fault? Had I known what was coming, I would have run.

Anna's eyes rattled me making me want to hug her, but I held back. Instead, I said, "I'm sorry. I know Meredith was a good friend."

Truman Blue had none of my human inhibitions. A natural therapy dog, he nestled closer to Anna, and wagging his tail leaned his warm body against her leg.

Running her fingers down his neck to his shoulder, Anna traced the outlines of the island-shaped black patches on Truman's gray fur. She stopped where the gray blended into a creamy-gold colored leg. The old woman's puffy hand moved to his head and gently stroked the dog's velvet-soft, tan and black speckled ears.

Truman was the king of dogs, at least in my opinion. Our connection transcended pet/owner. His easygoing personality inspired me to be more content and less judgmental. Pre-Truman, I spent too much time and money disguising my passage into being a-half-a-century-old. Now, my shoulder length light brown, gray streaked curls complimented the coloration expressed on his short fur. Handling my trained therapy dogs at nursing homes was my hobby and contributed to my appreciating my station in life.

"Blind, big, cozy," Anna said moving her finger over the ridge above Truman's one blue eye. Communication with Anna was problematic. Her memories and sentences vacillated between abrupt and elegant.

"He has two different colored eyes, one blue eye and one brown. That's just the color they are. He's only five years old and has no problem seeing. And, yes, I agree, he's a very big and cozy hound dog."

Anna pointed a thick finger toward my trainee.

"This is Judith. She's new in town. She wants to take her corgi on visits, so she's learning what we do. She'll bring her dog Gonzo with her the next time she comes here." Judith had visited once before observing my best friend Leslie and her dog Rusta, but Anna obviously did not remember her.

Judith stepped forward. "Nice to meet you. This seems like a pleasant place to live."

Anna eyed Judith, and her breath changed to a hoarse whisper, "Died too soon."

Therapy dog comfort-visits were supposed to be tranquil. I had expected a typical visit to teach our new volunteer the basics, but today was not normal. To begin with, when Judith joined me for today's training session, vanity crept in and challenged my confidence. Comfortably inconspicuous wearing my Peaceful Pets logoed polo shirt, khaki pants, and walking shoes, I was outshone by Judith who radiated the image of a dynamic banker. I knew she worked at a bank, but I was unsure if this was her normal public presentation or if she was turned out for effect. I reminded myself that I was the expert in training therapy dog teams and moved on.

Besides that slight bobble in confidence, Anna's agitation caused my intuition to scream out she was implying that something ominous, something malicious had happened.

Attempting to seize normality, I launched into coaching Judith. My trainees invariably took the brunt of my life-long drive to teach. "Truman loves when people touch him. Comforting a person is a collateral bonus to his receiving attention. You can't teach a dog to comfort people. You can only teach them to behave socially, according to human expectations. Not all dogs want to do therapy work."

"Gonzo likes attention from anyone," Judith said.

"That's great. It's important to remember to let the dog do the work. Don't think you are the most important team member. My real function is to be Truman Blue's chauffeur and social secretary and of course, his official leash holder. One of the residents here calls me Margie the Mutt Manager."

Judith scribbled in her half-full notebook, *let the dog do the work.*

"She's dead." Anna turned her head toward me, her neck emitting an arthritic pop. She raised her hand off the arm of her wheelchair, balled it as much as she could, and shook it at me as if she was thumping yeast dough.

Judith glanced at me and fidgeted.

My inner coach felt the need to advise my trainee. "Visits are usually low key, but sometimes they drain your emotions. Interacting with a lot of people tires a dog too."

"I hope Gonzo works out. I'm inspired to learn how to do this. I don't have a lot of experience comforting others, but this seems like a nice place to start," Judith said as she bent down to sniff a live hyacinth on a polished walnut end table.

For a town the size of the mini metropolis of Water Tree, Mississippi, Four Oaks Cottages was an upscale nursing home. 'Cottages' was a misnomer. The facility had 100 rooms. True to its name, the décor was cottage style, comfortable but prosperous cottage style. It was more like a cottage by the British definition rather than a small American bungalow. Four rotund oak trees dominated the front wrap-around porch, hence the name Four Oaks.

Anna grabbed Judith's hand, startling the trainee.

"She's dead, you know."

Judith slid her hand out of Anna's. "Yes dear, I know."

I continued. "Elder care is good here. When I visit a new facility, one thing I key in on is the plants used in the decor. When I see healthy live plants, my first impression is that the staff probably has good nurturing skills. The dusty plastic plants I see at some facilities tells me the staff doesn't have time to take care of the details, and management doesn't care enough to hire a good cleaning staff. When I get old and my health fails, I want someone who cares about details taking care of me."

A frowning nurse turned her head and hurried past us. "Dogs, bunch of hooey," she hissed.

I whispered, "Our nickname for that nurse is Lizzie Borden. She'll axe you in a minute if you don't follow protocols. Her real name is Nurse Connelly. If I were a resident here, I wouldn't want her near me. Steer clear of her. She's creepy."

Down the hallway, from room 201, an ambulance crew wheeled out a gurney carrying a sheet covered body. I wanted to tell Judith how a sheeted body marked my past trauma and made me dizzy, but I did not know her well enough to share past secrets. I slowly breathed in and out, trying to shake off the memory. There was too much disquiet today. I needed to truncate this visit without Judith realizing I was cutting it short.

Anna took my hand for an instant then dropped hers back in her lap. She shivered so hard her shoulders shook the wheelchair.

"Are you okay? Do you need a blanket?"

Anna's eyes flicked to the side. "She died wrong."

"Died wrong?" I had not intended to ask the question aloud.

Anna's disquieting persistence activated my favorite internal defense, the sarcasm gene. I wanted to ask, *so then she didn't go peacefully? Did she defy the rules of the art of dying? Or maybe like Alexander Hamilton, she was in an illegal duel to the death.* I shut my mouth before it got out-of-hand-outrageous and offensive.

I refocused my objective of raising Anna's spirits, but I was at a loss for appropriate words. I was never at a loss for words, only appropriate words. Anna always enjoyed hearing about Truman, so I fell back on my default of dog-talk. She had heard it before, but she would not remember. "Truman's a gem. He was one of six puppies in a rescued litter. His mother was a mix of Labrador, boxer, and pit bull. His dad was a Lab-bloodhound-greyhound mix."

A spark of curiosity flickered in Anna's tired eyes.

"He's such a handsome fellow. Are you sure he isn't purebred?" Anna asked. Fluidity of conversation waxed in and out for Anna.

"I'm sure. I had his DNA checked."

"He's a spectacular potpourri of colors," Anna said. She stroked Truman's multi-color coat. Her expressive thought reflected her earlier life as a literature professor at the exclusive Lorettina College for Women.

"Judith, one of the benefits of therapy dogs is they activate people's brains and connect them to the tangible world. Therapy dogs help relax and inspire people."

Truman rested his chin on Anna's lap, and his ears flopped out at right angles onto her fluffy pink robe. The dog's eyes rolled up toward her face, his eyebrows pleading for more petting.

Anna stroked the side of his face. Between blimp-like swells, her knuckles were narrow, like the joints of twisted animal balloons. I imagined as a young woman she had delicate hands that clicked keyboards and inspirited chalk to flow across blackboards. I wondered if it was steroids or disease causing her whole body to resemble a human-sized parade balloon.

With more dexterity than possible from a hand two sizes too thick, Anna touched a finger to Truman's cool shiny nose and traced the black blaze that ran up his cream-colored muzzle. Anna's finger stopped at the black widow's peak that pointed nose-ward from the cap-like patch between his ears.

More air than words, Anna's was almost inaudible. "The black one killed her."

I struggled to follow Anna's mood swings, and her death comments were making me cringe. *The black one? Seriously?* I had not pegged Anna as being racist but then our conversations had never been philosophical. I let it slide. At her age and condition, it was not a battle I could win. I reminded myself I was here to comfort, not confront.

Anna's eyes darted from side to side. She leaned forward in her wheelchair, bending as close to Truman's ear as her swollen belly would allow. Her eyes caught mine, and she whispered to the dog loud enough for me to hear, "The black one killed her, you know. Get help, please."

Anna rotated her head toward Judith.

Judith shrugged.

"When a resident asks for help, we're supposed to get it, no matter what," I said.

Nurse Connelly walked by again. I braced myself and stopped her. "Anna seems to think that her roommate died unnaturally. She's asking for help."

Nurse Connelly's eyes locked with mine. We nicknamed her Lizzie Borden, her stare looked like she was about to whop someone up the side of the head.

"I will take care of her," Lizzie said through her teeth. She patted Anna's arm, sneered at Truman and continued down the hallway.

My phone rang with the Leslie-specific ringtone, "How Much is the Doggie in the Window." My phone was usually turned off on visits, but I had forewarned Judith that I was anticipating a critical call. Leslie and her therapy dog Rusta had planned to join us at Four Oaks, but a doggie emergency waylaid them.

"Excuse me, Anna. Judith will talk to you for a moment," I said and grabbed my phone out of my tote bag.

"Are you sure it's okay?" Judith said, tilting her head toward the glowering Lizzie Borden.

I whispered, "It'll be fine. I'll be back in a minute. I hate to take calls, but this is important."

Judith nodded.

"Hi, Leslie," I walked down the hallway, tugging on Truman's leash. He pulled backward, not wanting to leave. It was against therapy dog regulations for me to hand him off to anyone else, so I insisted he follow.

"She's going to be okay. It's not bloat." Leslie choked on the words.

Leslie's phone transmission dropped for an instant then the signal picked back up. "... swallowed something when I walked her last evening, but I didn't know what it was. She grabs so much junk. I thought it was cat poop. It turns out it was one of those soft, spiky puffer balls kids get out of gumball machines. It went down okay, but it wasn't going to pass or let anything else pass. I'm on my way to the surgery clinic, but they're thinking they can get it with endoscopy. They won't have to cut her."

"Goofy chocolate Lab," I said. For more than one reason, I was glad my friend's dog would be okay. Leslie and I relied on each other for emotional support, and I was spent.

"Goofy, is hardly strong enough. Money pit is more like it," Leslie chuckled.

"But she's worth it," I said.

"Right, but sometimes..." Leslie grunted.

"Do you think she'll be well enough to do our hike this weekend?"

"I'll ask the vet and let you know by tomorrow. We may have to shorten it. Knowing Rusta, it won't take her long to bounce back from the anesthesia."

Unnoticed, Anna had wheeled up behind me. Truman jumped up and spun around as her wheel made contact with his tail. At the same time, Anna grabbed the edge of my blouse, scaring the life out of me.

"You and me, talk. Death. Bad. Murder." She hissed the last word from the back of her throat. She rolled her head over her shoulder toward where Lizzie Borden stood.

I put my hand on Anna's arm. "We can talk. I'll be off in a second."

From behind the nurse's station, Lizzie's eyes threw daggers. Sunlight glaring through the window caught her Connelly nametag and sent a light ray slicing across Truman's side. I turned away.

"I thought I heard murder. Is something wrong?" Leslie asked.

Great, I was in a three-way critical conversation I did not want overheard. I walked down the hall to the foyer. "It's Anna. She's upset because Meredith died. She insists Meredith was murdered."

"Do you think Anna's afraid of dying unexpectedly?"

"Maybe. But she did say murder. In my past three years visiting Four Oaks, Anna has never been this intense."

"What's your gut say?"

"My red flag didn't jump out of its bin and start waving in the sky, but I must admit her fixation on murder unnerves me."

"I seriously doubt Meredith was murdered. Stick to your job. If it is murder, Four Oaks will take care of it."

I took a deep breath. "Right, stick to being leash holder."

"Yeppers. Step back and let Truman do his thing."

Truman led the way back to Anna, and she reached out her thick hand putting it on the dog. Truman leaned against her and dropped his head, savoring the neck massage.

Anna's face sought mine. Her eyebrows rose, stretching the thin folds of eyelids that served as scaffolding for her eyes. I stiffened, anticipating another bombshell.

"Meredith, murder."

Judith walked up to us, so I redirected the conversation attempting to lead Anna back to what I believed was reality. "Meredith and Anna were roommates since Meredith arrived here a few months ago. She was a happy lady despite being sick. She came here with deep pneumonia, but I thought she was getting better. She crashed quickly."

Anna nodded, then shook her head no.

"Anna was a literature professor whose specialty was murder mysteries. She tends to be on the suspicious side," I said.

Anna glowered.

"You must have been very close to Meredith," Judith said.

"Yes, we lived together in the same room. Meredith would not give up. They didn't want her to get better, so they killed her," Anna said.

Was the old Anna back for the moment? Maybe partly back.

"Her body was fragile, wasn't it?" Judith asked.

"She was not well, but she didn't want to die. She liked me," Anna said.

"Why would someone want to kill Meredith?" I asked.

"Meredith said 'no.' The Black One said, 'No one says no to me.'"

"I'm sorry," I had nothing else to say. Judith appeared to be at a loss too.

"They killed them you know." The old woman persisted.

I expected odd trains of thought from residents but following Anna's irregular mental flow was like being a blindfolded passenger riding down an unfamiliar country road riddled with potholes.

I decided her change from singular to plural discredited the validity of her story. Inexplicably, my internal caution flag still flew yellow.

Chapter 2

My yellow flag turned orange when I caught site of Lizzie Borden stomping back my way. With each step her soft-soled shoes scrinched a half-squeak, half-plop, on the waxed floor.

She clutched Anna's wheelchair handles and shoved it forward. "Time to go," Lizzie said, pushing Anna off toward her room.

I considered saluting. Truman turned his head catching my eye, obviously thinking the same thing, rude woman. Most nursing home staffers are polite and business-like, some are laid back and casual, a few are strictly business. Lizzie pushed it a notch further and exuded militaristic. I wondered if Lizzie doubled as a hatchet woman or if in order to survive, she put a canyon of emotional distance between herself and the residents.

"Do you think there is any truth to what Anna is saying?" Judith asked.

"I'm pretty sure the nursing home staff doesn't kill people. Old people are their bread and butter. But there may be a few residents who are so aggravating, the thought of murder might flippantly cross a mind or two. I doubt any of this staff would take it so far as to murder someone."

"Probably not, but you never know. People have all sorts of motives for murder," Judith said, clicking a polished thumbnail against the likewise polished nail of her middle finger.

"It may happen in some places, but I can't imagine it happening here. If you visit a lot of facilities with Gonzo, you will see nursing homes come in all varieties. Some are plush with marble fountains in the foyers. Others are stark with hard cots and no pictures on the walls. In our four years of being therapy dog team partners, Truman and I have seen them all."

"I have seen a few visiting my extended family," Judith said. "This doesn't seem like a place of abuse, or murder."

"I agree," I said. "Truman rates this place high."

"Truman? How?"

"He determines how often we return to a facility. The ones that are offensive to my wimpy nose send Truman's quarter-bloodhound genes into aggravated overdrive. He heads toward the exit as soon as we arrive. I never force him to stay. He can't bring comfort if he is uncomfortable. A vigilant therapy dog handler does not subject a dog to discomfort. Truman loves this place."

Truman turned his attention to an old man sitting in a chair beyond the gap Anna's wheelchair had occupied. The dog's eyes pleaded with his signature look clearly stating, 'I'm such a deprived doggie. Can I please visit?'

I swept my hand forward toward the man and gave Truman the release, "Go visit." Truman sashayed up to the old man who was sitting in a bent-over-nearing-death posture. I recognized the neatly quaffed silver head as belonging to Mr. Robert Smith, an eccentric elder with a generic name. He was known to his friends as Bob.

Mr. Smith reached toward Truman, exposing a large gold Mickey Mouse watch on his wrist. He gently patted Truman's head, "Good, doggie," he crooned.

"Mr. Smith spends most of his time in the social areas. He doesn't like being alone in his room," I said.

"You must like people," Judith said.

Mr. Smith patted harder.

"Yes, I do, and dogs," he said.

I never understood why folks thought dogs liked to be patted on the head. Truman's eyes blinked with every pat indicating slight distress, but he stood stoically. He sensed when a person was trying to connect. He was emotionally generous and much more people savvy than most humans. My emotional support skills were uncouth compared to my dog. He never wavered.

"I like your watch," I said.

Mr. Smith lit up. "You like Disney?"

"Yes, I grew up watching Disney. I dreamed about a career as a Disney artist. I loved and still love all things Disney, especially the artwork."

"Me, too."

Mr. Smith's crooked stick fingers wriggled down Truman's neck to his shoulders. He shook his twig-like right index finger at me, "You better take care of this dog, he's special."

"Yes, he is special, he loves me, and I love him. We're tight buddies. We take care of each other."

The old man wrapped both fragile hands around my dog's head and scratched him under his jaw. Closing his eyes to a slit and tilting his head, Truman leaned into the scratches.

The old man once again raised a twig-like finger and pointed toward the direction Lizzie wheeled Anna. "She's right you know," he croaked.

"I beg your pardon," I said.

"She's right. They killed her."

"Why do you think that?" Judith asked.

"Meredith was getting well. She was going home to take care of her granddaughter. She wasn't ready to die."

I wondered how Mr. Smith's life had influenced his conclusion. I struggled to envision where he might have come from and who he had been in his early life. This decrepit man was once a teenager, physically fit, his life ahead of him. He survived the ups and downs of life. He survived the crazy stuff that teenagers do. I wondered about his love life. Was he once a wild gregarious young man, or a shy recluse? At ninety-something, his body was a shell left over from the life that preceded it. I wondered who he had been and how it shaped the thought that Anna was a victim.

"Who do you think killed her?" Judith interrupted my thoughts.

"I don't know who," he grumbled. In spite of his bent spine, he lifted his chin, and his upturned eyes linked with mine. "I only know it wasn't her time. I sense when folks here are about to pass on. They nick-named me Jan Smitharud." He giggled.

His change of moods disturbed me.

Truman's eyes flicked toward me. Was he assuring me that this man was telling the truth? Was he asking me if the grumbling man was still safe? I wished I better understood dog-speak.

The old man snickered. "You don't know if I'm senile or not, do you? Do you think I'm a crazy old man?"

His honest perception unsettled me. I went with my fallback, honesty. Truth was easier to track than lies. "I'm confused about your nick-name."

"You're too young to remember Stenerud."

"The name sounds familiar, but I can't place it."

"Wasn't he a football player? A kicker?" Judith asked.

"Jan Stenerud. Kansas City Chiefs, '67 to '79. Packers, '80 to '83, then to the Vikings. First placekicker in the Pro Football Hall of Fame."

"Ah, now I sort of remember. I'm not a huge football fan. Were you a football player?" I asked.

"No! You are dense, dear. They tease me about kicking them over the goal post! You know when a resident kicks the bucket? I flawlessly predict my co-habitants' deaths. At least when it's natural." His laugh split the air.

Judith giggled. "You're clever, Mr. Smith. I'm not sure if you're being truthful, but you are brilliant and a tease."

Mr. Smith leaned over and beckoned us closer to his wheelchair.

He whispered, "You want to know who's next?"

"I'm not sure I do," I said.

"Sure," Judith said.

I glared at her. She smiled back.

"Old Perkins, room 206. You watch. He won't make it through the night."

The hair on my neck prickled. I shivered, and a rush of goose bumps flew up my arms.

Head nurse Renee Blackwell appeared out nowhere. "Hi, Margie, Judith. It's time to gather up the flock for lunch. Margie, we would be glad to have you stay, but you know the health department won't let dogs in the dining room."

Renee scratched Truman behind the ear. "Who's a handsome goood dooogie? Judith can stay if she wants."

I tended to withdrawal when anyone asked me to join them for lunch. Two years ago, Sjogrens disease altered my eating habits. Out of desperation, I avoided certain trigger foods. "That's okay. I have strange eating requirements," I said.

"Most of our residents have unique dietary requirements. Accommodating difficult diets is one of our specialties," Blackwell said. She smiled a half-smile and walked off.

Judith scrunched her forehead. "I noticed her name tag, Blackwell. Didn't Anna say the black one murdered her roommate?"

The hair on my neck rose a second time. Judith's association made sense. Could Blackwell be the black one? Was Renee Blackwell a charlatan, a fake, a murderer? For what end? Murder tended to have something to do with money or jealousy. With old folks, money and inheritance were the most likely motives and in rare cases, hatred or bitterness might be the impetus. Blackwell did not seem hateful. Had she murdered Meredith for money? Why? How could that be?

"I don't know. I mean, yes that is what Anna said, and her name is Blackwell. But I can't imagine," I said.

"It's something to think about," Judith said.

"I prefer not to think about it. Our job is to bring comfort, not to investigate," I paraphrased Leslie's admonishment, but my curiosity reached out for more information.

"Are you staying for lunch? Do you want to take Gonzo on Janice's visit Thursday? You can take your dog on visits after today." I switched subjects avoiding the Blackwell question.

"I can't stay for lunch. Let's call it a day. And sorry, I can't make it Thursday. I have to be at work at the bank."

"Bank? Oh, yes you look like you're ready to go to work now."

Judith squinted. "What does that mean?"

"Oh, nothing." I gathered up my tote bag, tugged on Truman's leash and made for the door. The dog followed. He looked like he was thinking I was being unreasonable and abrupt, as well as rude. I was glad no one could read me as well as my dog.

Chapter 3

I loaded Truman into the back of my HRV and pulled out of the parking lot not sure of where I was headed. Not typically a retail therapy addict, the compulsion to shop directed my emotional GPS. I drove to embrace the transient sense of control that comes with purchasing something, anything. Buying things for myself was more of a chore than a pleasure but buying for my dog was entirely another matter.

We ended up at our favorite pup-shop, K9 Connections, a doggie superstore. Regulars called it Can-Con. I pulled into the parking lot, and Truman thumped his tail against the back of my seat. He wagged his whole body anticipating the treats liberally doled out by Can-Con's staffers. Truman always begged for treats as if he was never fed.

I opened the rear hatch and snapped on his leash. Truman disobediently jumped out before I cued him. Putting him back in the car for a re-do meant throwing a treat into the back of the car, which he might construe it as a reward. I huffed, admonishing myself to remember to watch him closer next time. I closed the hatch and headed into the store, Truman pulling me more than any respectable therapy dog should.

The automatic door slid open, and Truman lunged ahead.

He headed straight for the treat bins, but a gentle tug on the leash and a pat on my leg and he was back at my side.

Surrounded by treats, he switched into work mode, no doubt confident of an inevitable work for treats exchange.

I headed to the food bowl section of the store. Perhaps a new doggie bowl would be the right medicine to distract me from Anna's accusations.

"Margie!" A high-pitched nasal voice cut the air.

I cringed and braced for the inevitable boob-smashing hug. She grabbed me. This woman's mandatory much-too-long hugs were meant solely for intimidation. Suffocating in her hug, my meager female appendages forced me flat up against her, while her ample bosom conveniently protected her face at a distance from mine.

"Hi, Charlotte. Long time no see." *I wish it had been a longer time. I was enjoying the drought.* The thought rushed through my mind but respectfully lodged there without spilling out of my mouth. When she released me, I turned my head in time to see Inky lifting his leg on Truman.

"Stop! Charlotte, your dog is peeing on my dog!" I jerked poor Truman's leash and backed away from the buxom broad in an effort to keep my dog from defilement

"Oh, you silly baby," Charlotte reached down and scooped up the diminutive black carcass of curls with one hand. She perched him on her biogenic shelf and kissed him on the top of his head. "When he sees a big handsome dog like Truman, he gets in such a snit."

You think he's in a snit? You and that little dog are snit-sparks and I'm about to detonate. I pulled out my virtual duck tape and sealed my mouth. I do not condone violence toward dogs, but if I had a squirt gun, I would have soaked the little pee-body and his insensitive hugger-mom, too.

Truman leaned against my leg and yawned, his way of showing stress and seeking comfort. I stroked his neck.

"Honey," Charlotte began.

I love honey, but I abhor people calling me that, especially someone who considers herself the queen bee.

"Wait until you hear what I have planned," Charlotte continued. "You know the fun match we have planned, next week?"

I nodded. Leslie and I planned to attend the fun match, a veritable dog play day in the park, open to everyone.

"We will follow up with an event much bigger and better. It has been top secret until yesterday when I finally got the go-ahead from City Recreation. It's called Hound Dog Pawty in the Park. We'll do it during the Founders Festival! It will be a huge fundraiser for the Water Tree Dog Shelter. It will be fabulous, simply fabulous. Locally, I have commitments from OGO, the Obsessive Golden Owners Club, the Water Tree Purebred Dog Association, the Shepherd Dog Club of North Mississippi, Bully Boy Rescue, and the Southern Obedience Agility Club. Oh, yes and a dock dog trainer, too. They'll all have info tables and demonstrations. Driving in from Alabama we'll have a mounted canine search and rescue group."

She laid a hand on my arm and leaned forward. The dark-hearted little Inky lifted a lip, "And from Memphis, a canine police corp. We'll have Rescue Row where dogs can be adopted on the spot, references checked, of course."

"Sounds fabulous." Overwhelmed, I wanted to be impressed, but I suspected Charlotte had some alternative hidden agenda.

"And of course, I want to invite the cuddly canines of Peaceful Pets to set up a table. Would you? Could you?" She giggled, and Inky's curls vibrated.

I divorced my emotions from my intellect, took a deep breath, smiled and answered, "Sure, we will be there." *In spite of you and your little dog.*

I had to hand it to Charlotte, when she concocted and organized an event she engaged 200%. On the other hand, if someone requested her help with something that was not her idea, she verbally committed but never came through.

"I've got to run sweetie," Charlotte said. She put the black poodle down. He headed straight toward Truman who retreated behind me. I feared the spoiled brat would pee on me. Before my leg became victim, Charlotte headed for the door half dragging the dark fuzz-ball behind her.

Truman rolled his eyes up at me. I read them as, "Thank you mom."

I headed to the treat isle to locate a new flavor of mini treat to use in training. Truman flopped on the floor, owning his space and telling me he was bored with shopping. I searched the multiple shelves and noticed a brand that sported a black toy poodle identical to Inky. I would avoid that flavor like the plague. I did not harbor resentment against poodles. They could be great dogs. I abhorred owners who picked poodles to inflate their poofy egos and never taught the dogs manners.

"Poodles," I muttered with a growl.

"What's wrong with poodles?" A smooth masculine voice came from directly behind me.

I had not heard anyone walk up. Except for a two-second rise from his head, Truman gave no indication of someone intruding into my space. He twitched his nose back and forth to sample the scents, and then plopped his head back down. He had enough action for the day, if action described visiting a nursing home.

I whipped around and faced the bright black eyes and shiny button nose of a young Jack Russell Terrier who was secured by the nicely muscled arms of a tall man. The dog wiggled and squirmed. Her tail stuck out behind the man's elbow and wagged so fast it blurred. Jacks were the only breed I had ever seen whose tails move faster than the human eye tracked. The terrier's tail wag moved at warp nine. Accompanied by zero butt wag, a terrier tail resembled a metronome on amphetamines attached to a solid four-legged base. Of course, that base exploded into action the instant the Jack deemed appropriate.

It had been a long day. I disdained defending my current dislike of poodles. I reached out to scratch the dog under the jaw. "Cute pup."

The Jack Russell yelped a sharp play-bark and struggled to escape. She pushed as hard as she could against the man's chest. Truman sat up. Still a pup at heart, he welcomed the squirming dog as a potential playmate.

"Easy Ginger."

The man's full dark mustache twitched synchronously with the kissy noises he made with his lips. The dog locked her eyes on his face. She flicked her tongue, and it skittered over the stubble on his chin. She focused back on Truman and squirmed harder.

"Try again little girl," the man said, and made more kissy noises.

My instinctive man-evaluator kicked into action without my giving it permission and classified him as all around average, nothing spectacular, and nothing offensive. Nice mustache, though. He had patience. Positive reinforcement takes time and effort, but the dividends paid off.

My irises dilated, and I raised my defensive shield. *Not for you. He's gay or resolved in marriage.* The pain from my last bonding disaster was fresh.

Ginger fixated on the man's face and quit wriggling. "Good girl," more kissy noises, "good girl," more kissy noises.

Ginger kept her eyes on the man's face for three seconds, an eternity for a jumping Jack Russell. One last, "Good girl," and he slipped a treat in front of her nose. She lipped it from his fingers and after she swallowed, he placed her on the ground. She play bowed and lunged at Truman who stood up stiff legged, arching his neck and wagging his tail high over his back.

"Truman, stay." My dog shot me his pitiful, "Oh mom," face. He stood still but turned his attention back to the sparkler of a dog.

The man squatted down, and folded super-squirmer Ginger into sit position and held her there. A few seconds later, she quit trying to get up. "Can they say hello?" He asked.

"Sure."

The dogs butt sniffed, then spun and bounced as far as their six-foot leashes allowed.

Above the chaos, the man reached out his hand, "Hi, I'm Jerry."

"Margie," I said. I dodged Truman's sideways leap and avoided his almost yanking my arm out of its socket. "And Truman Blue."

Jerry cocked his head to the side like a curious dog. He smiled. "They look compatible. Do you want to give them a run in the play yard? I'm always looking for playmates for Ginger. I'll buy you a cup of coffee and we can watch while they run off some energy."

"Sounds good. It's either that or I might get my arm dislocated."

Jerry chuckled.

I guessed the reason I gave for accepting his offer was not a great compliment.

Jerry picked up Ginger and I told Truman to heel. We walked to the coffee bar at the back of Can-Con. On the wall above the coffee bar hung a colorful sign painted with playing dogs and the words, "K9 Connections: Where all the Pieces Come Together." I had seen it a hundred times, but was never sure what it meant.

Inside the play area, we let the dogs off their leashes. They took off running like old friends. A clear plastic half-wall surrounded the play area. Outside the wall, bistro tables surrounded the perimeter. Can-Com provided a fast food-like playground for dogs, with seating for coffee drinking doggie parents. Its nature-themed plastic elements were constructed for safety and sanitation. Flushable grid-covered drains surrounded artificial shrubbery.

The play elements mimicked agility course obstacles gone natural. Fake saplings lined with closely spaced artificial timbers guided the dogs into the back and forth motion of weave poles. In the middle of the playground, a hill made from sloping rocks led up to a flat hilltop and then back down toward a fake stream that led to a small pool. A mini-mountain A-frame and a plateau-like pause table enticed climbing dogs. Jumping logs and clumps of shrubs punctuated the floor and kept dogs from exceeding a safe speed. Four tunnels of different sizes ran under the artificial hills and mountains.

"Can you keep your eye on them for a moment while I order us coffee? Ginger should be okay unless she gets over stimulated. What would you like?"

Your body, popped into my head, but I had no trouble keeping that image to myself. It had been a long while since I had been with a man. My face heated up. I refocused on the board. "My favorite is Bark Chocolate Mocha Supreme, but I feel like trying something new." Was that a Freudian slip? I turned redder.

I snapped back. "A Salty Golden Caramel Latte, cashew milk, medium, please."

"One Salty, you got it. I'll bring it to the table."

I picked a table while Jerry ordered our coffees. Taking turns chasing each other, Truman and Ginger ran full blast around the playground. They splashed through the stream and Truman plopped down in the pool. Ginger yapped in his ear. He jumped up and they headed toward the tunnels.

Truman ducked into the largest tunnel, and Ginger flew into a smaller parallel tunnel. She exited first. Waiting at the opening of the big tunnel, she nipped at Truman's legs as he ran out. Truman leaped in the air, did a flying spin, and took off galloping.

I cracked up. What a hoot. I loved watching dogs play.

Jerry handed me my latte with his left hand and took the seat opposite me. "They must be doing okay, if you are laughing."

"What did you get for yourself?" He was not wearing a wedding ring, that talisman that wards off eager temptresses. I took a deep breath and reassessed. Across from me sat a gentle man who was attractive to me because he was a skilled dog handler and seemed safe. My previous choices of men had been poor. I had chosen men who were "interesting" and "risky." Safe was a male quality that eluded my past relationships. The result was I vowed never to commit to a man without a long front-side familiarity. This man excited me. If truth be told, I cared more about how a guy treated animals than his physique or sophistication. Experience had taught me to equate handsome with heart and actions, not with looks.

He cocked his head again and smiled. "You're thinking hard."

Crud, he's adorable. My cheeks heated again, and I hoped they were not red. I raised my cup with both hands to cover my flushing cheeks. "This tastes divine."

Jerry sipped his coffee, and I enjoyed his quiet slurpy noises. When he lowered his cup, a slight spattering of white frothy whipped cream freckled the tips of his mustache hairs.

I noticed his lips. I averted my eyes.

"A Brindle Frappuccino, white and dark chocolate swirl. It's tasty," he said.

"Cute," I said and put my cup back in front of my mouth. *Wrong choice of words, nitwit.*

"Tell me a little bit about yourself, Margie," Jerry said.

I liked the way he said my name. Now what? *Gay...think gay. The sweet guys are always gay...don't freeze.* I froze.

Ms. Sarcasm grappled for control and won. "I've been around for awhile. There's a lot to tell. I don't think we have that much time. I need to feed my dog soon," I said and wished I had not. I had uttered the canine-themed version of, 'I have to go wash my hair'.

Jerry cocked his head and grinned. "Let's talk about dogs. That should give us some common ground. Where did you get Truman?"

He recognized my nervousness which made me more nervous. He was sensitive. He was interested, rather than trying to prove he was interesting. That puppy-like head cock melted my heart. Asking a caninophile about their dog was as bad as asking a grandparent about their new grandbaby. I relaxed. I could talk dogs.

"A few years ago, I lost Timber, my soul dog. He was thirteen. I didn't think I would ever..."

Truman shrieked. Ginger had gripped one of his floppy ears in her teeth and was tugging.

Jerry jumped up and yelled in a voice that would bring down the walls of Jericho, "Ginger, NO!"

She let go. Truman ran toward me, tail tucked and looking back over his shoulder at Ginger. Jerry and I ran through the gate, and he grabbed up his dog just as she started to make a run for it. I knelt down by Truman and examined his ear.

"Is he alright? I'm so sorry," Jerry said.

"I think so." A trickle of blood oozed out of a small hole in his earflap. Truman leaned on me for comfort.

Ginger struggled to get down.

"No you don't, you imp. You have done enough damage for the day." He tucked her under his arm and reached his hand down to help me up.

"Why don't you drop by my office and I'll take a look at that ear and clean it up for you. No charge."

"No charge?" The question jumped out of my mouth before I could stop it. What would he charge me for? First aid supplies? I had my own, thank you. I huffed. *I knew you were too good to be true.*

He shook his head, wrinkled his forehead and shifted his eyes downward. "No, of course not."

Why did this guy think I would let him charge me to clean up my dog's ear? Only vets charged for pet-med. He was a sleaze bag. I opened my mouth to voice a sarcasm and stopped.

Three months ago, a new veterinarian bought old Doc Peterson's business. My critters were up to date on shots and had not needed vet care. This must be him. No wonder he handled his dog so well.

"Sorry, I didn't mean to offend you. I guess we never got that far with our introductions. I'm Jerry Elliston, I'm the new vet in town."

A vet. Score! Once again, my unfaithful cheeks flamed. *Gay, think gay...nice guy, possible friend, nothing more.* And then stupid took over. "The new vet's name is Howard."

Jerry chuckled. "It is, but don't remind me. I'm not fond of my given name, Howard Jerald Elliston, the third. Please, call me Jerry."

I followed Jerry's yellow Jeep to his office. He led the way to the side door and held it open for Truman and me. Inside, a gorgeous woman in a white medical coat stood holding a stethoscope. Her nametag read Lynn Elliston.

He's taken. Not gay. Not a chance for me here. No ring had thrown me.

"Jerry, I'm glad you dropped in." The woman's smile accentuated her no-need-for-make-up natural beauty. "Can you take a look at a cat that came in? She has skin irritation and I'd like your opinion."

"I will be glad to, but I need to check out Truman's ear. This little imp," he patted Ginger on the shoulder and the dog reached up and licked his chin, "decided to play tug-o-war with this hound's ear."

"Ouch," said the lovely lady.

"Lynn, this is Margie."

Lynn grasped my hand in a firm handshake, "Nice to meet you."

"You too," I responded, but her elegant beauty unnerved me.

"Lynn's my assistant." Jerry's face turned Cheshire Cat.

Of course, and what does she assist you with? My mind chattered caustically.

"Assistant? You cad." Lynn flicked Jerry's arm.

They were tight. I was unmistakably out of my league. I did not intend to duel for this vet's attention with this runway-model partner gone vet tech.

"I hate to admit it, you are good," Jerry grinned.

"Oh?" I slipped. *Idiot.* I hoped he would not elaborate.

"She's my coworker, and my sister, too. Very competent."

For an instant, my inner self lurched off the side of the road into an embarrassment ditch.

"After all these years, my big brother still likes to give me a hard time." Her face wrapped with mock animosity, Lynn put her hands on her hips. "I am NOT his assistant. I too, am a full-fledged vet. I only work part-time because I'm working on a doctorate in animal behavior."

"She wants to be a dog shrink," Jerry said.

"You analyze couch potato pups?" I was back in my lane.

"I'm focusing on converting aggressive dogs."

"Oh, then civilizing Chihuahuas?"

"Sometimes," Lynn chuckled.

"Hey, I like the little guys," Jerry said, feigning insult.

"Speaking of which, I need to go take Poncho's vitals."

"Please take this urchin with you. I'll take a look at the cat after I tend to her victim's ear."

In the exam room, Jerry dropped to one knee to get a close look at Truman's injury. "Not too bad. It broke open enough that it should drain, and it's not totally through his ear. I'll clean it up and give you some ointment to keep it clean. That should be enough." He scratched Truman's neck. "Poor fella, bad Ginger played too rough. You are a sweet boy."

Truman leaned against Jerry to absorb more affection. I envied the relaxing massage from Jerry's hands.

"I need to go help Lynn with the scaly cat. I would love to get together with you to finish a cup of coffee, or have dinner. Could we do that?"

Panic. *Was he asking me for a date? He was asking me for a date.* My mind went warp speed to 13-year-old boy-girl chaos. What was wrong with me? Sarcasm stepped in and made itself audible. "You want to make up for your dog ruining my expensive cup of coffee?"

"I take that as a no."

"No. I mean, yes. Not..."

I took a slow deep breath and relocated my adulthood. "Sorry, When?"

His eyes twinkled. "I'll need to check my schedule, but soon. Right now, I have to take care of that cat. Can we exchange phone numbers?"

"Sure."

We shared phone info and I headed home. It was not the first time I embarrassed myself. I was one-hundred percent confident it would not be the last.

Chapter 4

Leslie and Rusta joined Truman and me at the Bullard Park for a combo of exercise, dog training and companionship. We headed around the eight-acre Erin Dan Lake with Truman and Rusta on long leashes hooked to harnesses. The dogs forged ahead with Leslie and me following at a quick-walk. The air was cool enough for an early Mississippi spring. Preoccupied with keeping the dogs' leashes from tangling while they romped, we could not finish a sentence. The two dogs play-growled, mouthed and bumped each other for ten minutes, and then relaxed into shoulder-to-shoulder slow dog trot.

"Leslie, I'm concerned about and odd conversation I had with Anna when Truman and I were visiting Four Oaks," I said.

"Aren't there usually odd conversations when we take our dogs to visit nursing homes?"

"This one was exceptionally odd."

"Like how?"

"Do you remember on the phone I told you Anna said Meredith was murdered? she was really upset."

"Of course Anna was upset. They roomed together."

"Yes. But Anna kept harping on how Meredith died. It gave me the creeps. She claimed Meredith was murdered by the black one."

"Did you mention it to anyone?" Leslie asked.

"Yes, Nurse Connelly, the one we call Lizzie Borden."

Leslie groaned. "That must have gone over like a lead balloon."

"Right. That new recruit Judith was with me and she heard it all. She suggested that the black one could be Nurse Renee Blackwell."

"Not likely. Blackwell seems sane to me."

"I agree. But it was all so weird."

A van pulled up as we neared the playground. The van doors opened, and two moms and five kids emerged. The kids ran to the playground.

Truman jumped up and down on the end of his leash wanting to join in.

"I don't understand his fascination with children," I said. "He's not around them much. My only child is a 6' 4" tall software tech who lives in Butte, Montana. Truman was terrified the first time he came eye-to-eye with a little human. He was only about 15 weeks old, and I had only had him a couple of weeks."

"He was still getting adjusted to his new home. How did he go from terrified, to adoring kids?"

"The kid's mom let me encourage Truman and the little boy loved on him. Ever since then he has absolutely adored kids."

"He has to like kids to work that crowd at Safe Acres Children's Shelter," Leslie said.

"It's one of his favorite places. He is so gentle with the little ones."

"I'm glad you opened that world for him. The Safe Acres kids always need cheering up."

The children spotted the dogs. They stopped playing and ran to the railroad ties that edged the playground. Smiles lit their faces, and the younger ones clapped their hands and tried to whistle.

"Wanna go let the dogs get some kid-training?" I asked.

"Sure."

We approached the two women who had brought the kids.

"Hi, I'm Margie and this is my friend, Leslie. We are members of Peaceful Pets, a pet therapy group. We are always looking for training opportunities. Would it be okay if your kids petted our dogs?"

The five kids formed a horseshoe around their mothers, listening for permission.

"Sure," said the mom with red hair.

The kids lunged forward.

I put my hand up in the universal stop signal. "Please, wait a minute. Let us get them in sitting position. Please stand where you are, and we will let them come to you, one at a time. Is that okay?"

The kids nodded.

"Truman, sit."

My dog sat.

"Rusta, sit." Rusta picked up her forepaw and leaned into her collar but did not sit. Her tail wagged hard, taking her butt with it.

Slightly amused, I waited while Leslie got her dog's attention.

"This is how we train," I said to the women.

"We hope," Leslie said.

"Our dogs will test our limits. Rusta isn't trying to be bad, she's challenging Leslie and trying to act as leader. Rusta knows Leslie wants to go see the children, she just wants to be in charge and skip a step in the introductions."

"Rusta, SIT!" Leslie's voice was lower and a little more insistent. Rusta sat.

Leslie and I waited for a few seconds before releasing my dog. "Truman," I pointed to one child and said in a cheery voice, "Go visit."

Leslie followed suit and released her dog. Rusta rushed forward and poked her nose rudely into each child's face or tummy, depending on whether the child's last meal had ended up in their mouth or on their shirt. The kids giggled.

Leslie pulled Rusta back and made her slow down.

Truman was more respectful, standing quietly until I signaled him to move on. He stepped up to a boy who was barely past toddler and was at eye level with my tall dog. The boy reached out his two chubby hands and cradled Truman's head. He planted a kiss on his shiny black nose.

"Aw," crooned both moms.

As usual, Truman flopped on his side then rolled to his back and stuck his forelegs straight out. I was not sure when he did this if he was demonstrating, "I promise not to hurt you," or if he was thinking, "You diminutive human, you are my servant, rub my belly!"

Rusta stood by a little red-haired girl who giggled as she ruffled the dog's brown ears. I loved watching dogs that loved kids. Dignified old dogs turn into puppies around children. Uninhibited affection is harder for humans. Our dogs inspired us to be more open.

"Such sweet dogs. Hi, I'm Tara," the red-haired woman said.

The shy boy skipped over and huddled under the shorter woman's arm like a chick under a hen's wing. "Hi, I'm Susan," the woman said.

"We appreciate you letting your kids pet our dogs. We don't have small children so it is helpful when we can round up kids to pet them. We do ongoing training to keep them familiar with all sizes of people," I said.

"It's our pleasure. The kids are totally entertained. The dogs are so well trained. I've always wondered how hard it is to give up a dog after you spend so much time training it. Will they be guide dogs?" Susan asked.

Leslie jumped in, "They aren't service dogs. They are our personal pets. These are therapy dogs and have a different job than service dogs. We visit people who are lonely or hurting physically or emotionally. We go to places like nursing homes, hospitals, rehab facilities, mental health facilities, and children's shelters. Therapy dogs work with their owners to serve other people. Service dogs are trained for a specific task to serve one person."

Susan pushed her toddler on the swing-set. "I see."

"My husband Ben's niece is in a children's shelter," Tara said. "We hope to adopt her, but we're trying to resolve some legal issues. The poor girl has had a rough life. Ben's sister and her ex-husband adopted her as a newborn, and a year later, the husband left them."

"The creep," Susan said.

"Ben's sister died five years ago and his mother has cared for the girl since then. Technically, Ben is not a legal blood relative, but Carley is part of our family. Because of the legal issues, the girl is at the shelter until we get the papers in order. Some issues are under court secrecy, so we don't know the exact problem. Hopefully she can move in with us within the next week or two."

"How kind and compassionate of you," I said. I was always amazed when people unloaded to a Peaceful Pets team. Most of us were not formally trained as counselors, but our dogs elevated us to the status of safe confidantes.

Tara grinned. "She is the sweetest twelve-year-old I ever met. It would be a blessing to add her to our home. As a plus, she said she would babysit for us, free." She gave a light head-noogie to the girl tucked under her arm.

"I like Carley," the little girl said.

"Truman loves visiting one of the local children's shelters. We're going there the day after tomorrow. The folks there do a good job taking care of the kids," I said.

"Which one are you going to visit?" Tara asked.

I was glad she brought it up. "Safe Acres."

"That's where Carley is!" Tara smiled broadly. "If you see Carley, tell her we love her! We text all the time, but it will encourage her if she hears it from someone else."

"Done," I said, happy to spread the love.

The kids became bored with the dogs and opted for the tube-slide and teeter-totter. Leslie and I headed north to finish our walk around Erin Dan Lake. We reached the last public restroom before the path led into a half-mile stretch of forest trail.

"I need to make a pit stop. Can you hold Rusta?" Leslie asked, handing me the Labrador's leash.

Leslie headed up the sidewalk to the small sandstone building. On the other side of the path, at the water's edge, a dark-skinned woman was elbow deep in the lake. I recognized her as Janice Klein, Bullard Park's stick-thin naturalist gardener. She was pulling invasive water plants and stuffing them into a black garbage bag. Janice was friendly with people but a relentless machine when it came to weeding. The park was her baby and no exotic invasive plant that attacked her terrain would live to tell about it. The park staff called her Plantinator after the cyborg assassin.

I met Janice and Soulman when she joined Peaceful Pets the previous year. Soulman was an amazing creature. His natural dog behavior and long silver schnoodle bangs disguised the fact that his diseased eyes had been removed, probably because of severe glaucoma. He was a FORD, found-on-road-dog. Janice was dedicated to being his seeing-eye person. Together they became an effective team that encouraged the life-challenged people they visited as a therapy team. What people did not see were the private moments when Soulman's loving comfort soothed Janice in her darker times. Janice struggled with depression. I was glad that Soulman and Janice had each other.

I wandered down the short hill to the lake edge to chat with Janice and let the dogs dabble their paws in the water.

"Hi, Janice."

Janice let go of the plant she was annihilating and sat back on her heals. She pulled off something I could only describe as her arm waders. The rubber gloves went to her armpits and connected with a strap across her back. She wiped perspiration off her face, leaving a few small streaks of pond scum in its place.

"Hi, Margie, Truman, Rusta. Great to see you. Where's Leslie?"

I nodded my head toward the restroom building.

Rusta air-scented a wide, thick patch of horsetail and river reed growing on the lake bank.

"Careful, there is a mallard hen and her chicks in there."

Rusta morphed into full alert, quaking in anticipation.

"Rusta, sit," I sternly commanded. The dog simulated sitting position, but remained on tippy-toes, front and rear. Her butt hovered inches from the ground. Shivers vibrated through her body from her nose out her tail.

Truman cocked his head and followed Rusta's fixated stare.

I wrapped both leashes around my hands several times and squatted down next to Rusta for better control. I was glad to hear the restroom door bang. I goofed. I stood and I said to Rusta, "Your momma is on the way down here, don't you dare bother those ducks."

As if the word "ducks" magically conjured the fowl from their hiding place, swimming at top speed the hen led her six half-grown ducklings out of the reeds. At that same instant Rusta launched herself into the lake. Of course, in true pack fashion, Truman followed. The dogs were off. In classic dumb dog handler fashion, I held on to the leashes and after two clumsy running steps, ended up face-first-belly-flopped in the lake.

I lifted myself in a soggy push-up and heard Leslie screaming her dog's name. Janice yelled for Truman. By the time Leslie made it down to us, Janice was sitting on the ground laughing so hard she could not talk. I brushed my hair out of my face. Duckweed entangled my saturated curls. Leslie dropped down next to Janice and they both cackled, gasping for air.

I crawled out of the lake and hauled myself to my feet, dripping with water and lake bottom sludge. I took a deep breath, "Truman, COME!"

He lifted his chin off the water and glanced back at me.

"TREAT!"

The dogs ruddered their tails and headed toward shore. It was a bad handling technique, but this was a near emergency.

Leslie snorted between chortles, "So...glad...I went...potty first...."

Janice and Leslie launched into a fresh set of uncontrollable howling. Red-faced, they leaned against each other convulsing.

The dogs reached the shore and Rusta ran straight to Leslie. Truman followed. The waterlogged dogs shook hard, saturating my two amused amigas. The women jumped up to get away from the ever-so-happy, sopping wet dogs. It was my turn to laugh. The dogs rubbed and rolled on the ground to dry themselves and then tried to rub on us. We sobered and pushed them away.

"Thanks for the comedy break, but I've got to get back to work." Janice donned her arm waders and returned to the lake.

"I need to get cleaned up. We've known each other for about six months now, and I don't think you've been to my house. Do you want to go with me to clean up?"

"That sounds wonderful."

Chapter 5

Leslie followed me to my house. I cleaned up and dried off my dignity. Leslie and I retired to my covered deck to munch crackers and pimento cheese dip and drink homemade lemon-limeade.

"You really have a nice place."

"I wish I owned it. My landlords, Jeanine and Rocky, are the best, but they would never consider selling it. I would buy it in a minute if it was for sale."

"Is the rent high?"

"Not bad, but I have to work to pay some of it."

"What kind of work do you have to do? Is it hard?"

"I guess it's hard, if you consider bottle feeding baby goats, brushing horses, and playing with dogs hard work."

"Sounds treacherous." Leslie drained her glass.

"Do you get to use the tractor?"

"I haven't yet. Rocky likes to mow. That's his thing. But sometimes I have to ride a horse and check out the 200 acres of woods."

"Horrible." Leslie chomped a cracker and wiped a bit of cheese from her lip.

"I do have to weed my own section of garden, and then eat the fresh produce."

Leslie pointed to the pasture on the other side of a hedgerow. "That's harsh. Hey, are those the baby goats? They are so adorably tiny!"

"Yes, Jeanine bought them to do goat yoga. They are Nigerian dwarf goats, the smallest of the small."

"Please don't tell me that the chestnut color one is Tyrion..."

"Okay, I won't. And I won't tell you the others are R2-D2, Tangina, and Thumbalina."

"Since they're dwarfs, is that politically correct?" Leslie asked.

I shrugged. "I didn't name them. Jeanine's husband Rocky did, and he isn't famous for his PC. Jeanine and Rocky are out for the day, so I'll be giving them their bottles in about an hour. You can help if you want."

"What fun! Don's not back until about 10 tonight, so I can stay a while."

"You can help with the evening feeding, too, if you like. I have to feed the four kids, six ponies, two horses, four King Charles Spaniels, three cats, two dwarf Scottish Highland cattle and one miniature donkey named Don Quixote. Plus mine, Truman and Caravaggio."

At the mention of his name, Caravaggio who was curled up in my lap, licked a white kitty paw and wiped his white cheek, reverse-fur, down to his black mustache. He rested his black-goateed chin on my thigh, relaxing with a resonating purr.

The donkey brayed, then turned and trotted off.

"Don Quixote! He's delightful," Leslie said.

"He looks cute, but he is DonQui through and through," I said. "He has decided that the little spaniels are his windmills."

"Oh, no."

"Oh, yes. I'm sure he would stomp them to death if he had a chance. Hence the low, hotwired fence around the donkey's pasture."

"Those spaniels aren't the most threatening of windmills."

"You got that."

"Speaking of mills, the rumor mill has it that something's up with you and the new vet, Dr. Elliston."

I almost choked on my drink. "What?"

"Do you deny having a Can-Con date with him?" Her eyes twinkled.

"No! I mean yes, yes I deny it."

"I understand that's how Truman got this hole in his ear that you haven't mentioned." Leslie glided a finger over the bump on my dog's ear.

"I met Jerry at Can-Con, and our dogs wanted to play. We had a cup of coffee to bide the time. His dog got overly excited and chomped Truman's ear, so Jerry cleaned it up for me. A tiny hole. No big deal. AND it was not a date."

Leslie squinted one eye. "Jerry? Not Dr. Elliston?"

I poured more lemon-limeade. "Drink up and forget it."

Leslie threw her head back laughing. "The lady doth protest too much. He's the vet that sent Rusta to the specialist when she swallowed that spiky ball. He seems like a nice guy."

"I'm not in the mood for another relationship. The last one screwed me up for the rest of my life."

"You are going to have to get over Mr. X someday." Leslie knew that I refused to mention my ex's name, and she played along.

"I wish I could. It's hard when your spouse dumps you because you have an incurable illness. I thought it was through sickness and health, death do you part."

"And he did the death thing, himself," Leslie added. "How long has it been?"

"Seven years."

"Don't you ever get lonely? Surely you want to have a close relationship with a human."

"I think about it every once in a while. But Truman fills most of the gaps. I enjoy my alone time, and I have my friends. It's not like when I was younger and wanted to grow up, get married and have a family. I'm content sitting here enjoying the beauty of the earth or doing my art stuff. I'm satisfied."

"Yes, but Truman isn't human. Close, but not quite. Same-species companionship is nice."

Leslie and her husband Don had moved to Water Tree six months ago. I met her when she brought her active Labrador to me to get certified as a therapy dog. We hit it off immediately. "Relationships are wonderful when they're with folks like you, who truly care. When you're trapped in a relationship that is unhealthy for all concerned, it is not nice. I prefer being alone to being emotionally smashed."

"Since we're friends, can I ask you a hard question?" Leslie asked.

I groaned. "You want to open my wounds?"

"Not exactly. I think it would be good for you to talk about your past."

"I'm ready. Ask away."

"Were you sad when he died?"

"I had mixed feelings when he crashed that stupid Piper into the side of a mountain. I may have felt differently if he hadn't had his girlfriend with him. We were in the process of divorce. I think I felt sorrier for his girlfriend. They were on their way to Mexico."

"He doesn't sound like a great husband."

"Most of the time he was insensitive and controlling, but he provided for our needs and some luxuries. He was a decent husband occasionally. He wasn't a horrible father to Morgan. Sometimes he tried to work on having a good relationship, but I guess he was so insecure he wore psychological heavy armor all the time. It kept him cold and distant."

"A knight in rusty armor?" Leslie asked.

"You could say that. Or the Tin Man who never found a heart. Insecure made him insincere. I always had to carefully think about how what I said would affect him and what he might do to retaliate. I was always walking on eggshells."

"Why on earth did you marry someone like that?"

"I don't know. I was in love with the idea of love rather than being in love with the man. He checked off the boxes on my wish list. Handsome, self-made, gainfully employed. Emotionally, I think he was a complete charlatan, and I didn't recognize that until it was too late. Even with his occasional stab at trying to have a satisfying marriage, the longer we were married, the more of a jerk he became. I was pretty depressed right before he died."

"I'm glad I met you post Mr. X."

"Yep, me too."

"So you are saying you don't miss being married?" Her statement was a question.

"I wish my marriage was something I missed. I ended up with the better end of the deal. It was divorce by death. His death kept me from the stress and stigma of divorce, although in our minds and hearts we were already divorced. Since we were at the beginning of legal agreements, we hadn't told our son. Even as an adult, Morgan still thinks his dad and the woman were on a business trip."

"I'll keep your secret. What bothers you the most about all that?" Leslie said.

"A couple of things. When I went to identify his body, that's when I first learned he was with someone when he crashed. It didn't seem out of the ordinary because he told me he was going on a business trip. At the morgue, when they pulled the sheet back for me to identify him, they realized they had pulled out the body of the wrong plane crash victim. She had nothing to do with his business. I worked with her at the school. That's when I put it all together. I had heard gossip but didn't know it was my husband she was involved with. I am sure they were running off to get married, even before our divorce. The doctor apologized profusely, but the image of betrayal was burnt into my memory."

"That's horrible."

"It did make it a little easier to ID his dead body. I was already numb and angry."

Leslie nodded her head.

"Realistically, it should have been okay. Two more weeks and we would have been in divorce court. I'm pretty sure if we had gotten divorced, I never would have received the money he promised. I'm sorry he had to die, but his insurance gave me a clean slate. He paid off all the bills postmortem."

Leslie nodded. "If it had been me, I would have smiled all the way to the bank. His misfortune gave you a small fortune tied with a bow of freedom."

"Fortune is stretching it. I ended up with enough to compensate for my inability to work full-time. I limit myself to living off the interest and dividends. I'm set for emergencies. I could work part time, but I never know when I'm going to have a flare. Sjogrens is the pits. Speaking of which, my eyes are getting dry. I need to get my drops and throat spray. I love being outdoors but it dries me out more than indoors."

"Let me refill our plates while you do that," Leslie said.

"I'll grab some t-r-e-a-ts for the dogs while I'm inside. Someday they are going to learn to spell and we'll have to rotate descriptive phrases so that they don't react to any one word."

"Like la petite nourriture?"

"If you say so."

Later that evening, we watched the setting sun turn the sky pink, purple, orange and yellow. Leslie left when the stars came out. It was nice to have company.

Bright moonlight shining through my bedroom window kept me awake. My thoughts went to Leslie. She was a good person. She tolerated my unpredictable moodiness. She never complained about the changes in my daily functionality and schedule caused by flares of Sjogrens Disease, a sister disease to Lupus. I expected the stresses of earlier today might bring on one of those flares. Stress did not have to be huge to bring on a flare, but the dump in the lake and revisiting my past might be enough.

The next morning, I woke up and felt a familiar burning sensation on my lower legs that signaled the start of a flare. I knew I had to be reclusive and take the day off from physical activity, or I would end up in a full-blown flare.

I peeked out my window to make sure Jeanine and Rocky were back. They were. I did not have to feed today. Terrific fatigue squelched all desire to do anything. Sjogrens would strike full force if I pushed myself. My joints would feel on fire, my brain would be fog-clogged, my eyes would be so dry they would stick to the insides of my lids, and my teeth would stick to my cheeks. If I tried to hold a conversation, my throat would enflame from lack of lubricating saliva. I did not need to be talking to anyone. My body needed re-coup time.

Sometimes flares lasted half a day, sometimes a month. Sometimes I could almost ignore them and carry on with my regular functions. Other times I could not leave the house, or get out of bed. A full-blown autoimmune flare felt like a killer flu without the vomiting or respiratory issues. In a full-blown flare, I did not have the energy to think. My cozy dog, Truman, was always my best company.

Staying at home and resting usually kept the flare at a low level, so I decided to binge watch *All Creatures Great and Small*. I drank quarts of water, ate a ton of fruit, napped three times, and checked my email. Truman hung out with me all day. By seven that evening, I was ready for bed. That was how flares rolled.

I slept until seven in the morning, when Truman pawed my arm indicating that his breakfast was long overdue. I didn't have much energy, but I was less exhausted than the day before. The skin on my legs no longer burned, an indication I was on the mend. I hoped I could keep my appointment at Safe Acres in the afternoon.

I fed Truman and Caravaggio. My phone reminded me I was on the schedule for the noon goat feeding. Jeanine and Rocky were only gone for the afternoon and would be back home to do the evening bottles. I fed myself breakfast and slogged down two tall glasses of water dashed with lime.

I streamed an episode of Hinterland. Truman pawed my leg, indicating he was bored. It was warm outside, so I took him up to Jeanine's huge heated pool and threw tennis balls. Playing pool fetch took minimal energy from me and expended a lot from Truman. As a bonus, the pool laundered my dog, saving me the efforts of giving him a pre-visit bath. It seemed like a great day to sit in the shade and read a book poolside, but my wet dog proved otherwise. In spite of covering myself with a large beach towel, Truman's vigorous shaking soaked me every time he emerged from the pool. I never understood why a dog seemed obliged to approach its human to shake off water.

Chapter 6

I arrived at Safe Acres and met up with Janice Klein and Soulman the blind schnoodle. We took a quick detour to the field adjacent to the parking lot so the dogs could do their thing before we went inside. The kids had the day off from school, so the four of us were today's entertainment.

"Thanks for changing your plans and volunteering as a second team," I said as we headed to the building.

"I'm not sure what to expect. Do you think the kids will be wild?" Janice asked. She drew her bottom lip under her top teeth. This was their first visit to Safe Acres. Janice's constant protective vigilance kept Soulman safe. Too much activity around her dog exhausted her.

"I don't know. If they make Soulman nervous, feel free to leave. He is your primary responsibility. Truman and I visit here once a month. There's a high turnover. Each time, there is usually a new group of children. They can only stay here 45 days. The kids are usually well behaved but get bored with the dogs after about an hour. They like to see Truman do tricks."

"Soulman knows a few tricks, and I brought his brush. Do you think the kids will want to brush him?"

"Probably. It depends on the kids. It really varies. There might be some who are overly active and some who just sit and say nothing."

"Soulman loves my sister's kids. I don't. Well, I guess I do, but they get on my nerves. I don't think I will ever have kids."

"Truman loves to be around kids. I only had one and he was sort of an accident. For a long time, I wished I had more kids. It was almost as if I mourned them because they were not being born. Then one day I realized I never would have more children, but my life was still satisfying"

"I feel that way most of the time."

"I justify it by remembering that I don't have to worry about how my non-existent children would be impacted by the hardships of the world."

"When we dream about having children, we don't dream about them being hurt by the world, but everyone is."

"I worry enough about my one son and my dog. It terrifies me to think of what could happen if Truman got lost, or if something happened to me. I wrote a will that leaves my meager savings and my pets to my son. He loves critters."

"Not a bad idea," Janice said. "You never know when it's your turn."

We walked up the sidewalk to the front door, making sure our dogs did not water the landscape shrubs.

"There's a girl here that I promised I would give a message to. Her name is Carley."

"What's she in for?" Janice asked.

"She's not 'in for' anything, except bad circumstances. These kids aren't the ones who messed up. It's a kind of limbo for them. They're here because for one reason or another, a parent can't take care of their kids."

"Collateral damage?"

"Yes. The children are here to wait out the next step in their capsized lives. There are hundreds of reasons kids land here. The parents are often the culprits. Drugs, neglect, imprisonment, abuse are all reasons these kids are here. Some folks shouldn't have kids. Some kids are waiting between foster homes. Others, like Carley, end up here because of tragedy and legal matters."

"Sad," Janice said.

"Do me a favor, don't share the info that I know about Carley. You never know how that might go over with the administrators here. Would you be able to occupy the younger kids while I try to give Tara's message to Carley? The houseparents keep a close eye on their charges and are suspicious about outsiders. They'll be watching you and Soulman closer than Truman and me because they know us."

"Sure, we can occupy the young ones. No problem."

We entered the activity room. Printed with letters in primary colors, the carpet was worn but clean. Books, game boxes and toys occupied shelves stacked halfway to the ceiling. For a place that housed children it appeared a bit too organized. On our last visit, the kids told me they cleaned up before and after we came. The kids loved to brush Truman and he obliged by shedding.

Six children were scattered around the room, two look alike brothers, around six and nine years-old and an apparent brother sister combo around ages four or five. The girl I assumed was Tara's niece and a 16ish girl sat on the sofa watching The Princess Diaries. By the looks on their faces, I guessed they would have preferred something a bit edgier.

All eyes turned to us as we walked in.

"Hi, I'm Margie. My dog is Truman. This is Janice and Soulman. We thought you might enjoy a visit from our dogs today. Would you like to pet them?"

The younger kids squealed and clapped their hands.

"Why don't you take Soulman over there," I said, pointing to four younger children playing with a wooden train set. "I'll sit with the young ladies, here."

Truman's size could intimidate small children. Normally, I made slow introductions to alleviate their fears. The un-intimidated four-year-old was quick. While I signed in, she ran up, threw her arms around Truman's neck and squeezed hard. My handler error embarrassed me and I appreciated my even-tempered dog.

"Be careful sweetie, you might scare him. Please let go and I'll show you the best way to greet a dog." For her future safety, I exaggerated. Truman loved kids and their impulsive natures. I seriously doubted any hug would ever scare him.

"Big doggie!" The girl hugged hard, and Truman rolled his eyes up to meet mine. I smiled and gave a short nod, my silent signal indicating he was being a good dog. The girl let go. The housemother collected the girl and walked her over to the group of younger children where Soulman and Janice held court.

"Brush him like this." Janice demonstrated to the six-year-old, the proper way to follow the grain of Soulman's coat. The younger kids obviously enjoyed brushing and giving Soulman belly rubs. Twenty minutes later, the novelty of the dog wore off. The two younger children left the room in search of a new distraction. Janice shared stories with the two who stayed.

The 16-year-old smiled when Truman leaned into her, soliciting neck scratches.

"He's adorable," the older girl said.

"Loveable," Carley said.

The ever-present housemother monitored our conversation from far enough away to appear she was not eavesdropping. I hesitated to share the message from Carley's Aunt Tara. The message was innocent, but legal stuff stuck to these kids like cockleburs and made normal conversation rough.

"Do you like my polish?" The older girl wiggled toes sporting sparkly blue toenails, protruding from strappy sandals. We chatted nail fashion, or rather, the girls chatted nail fashion. I folded my hands to hide my rough cuticles and uneven, unpolished nails. I listened, but the girl sensed I was a lost cause. She got up and left the room, leaving Carley and I alone on the sofa.

"You are Carley, right?"

The houseparent perked up. No doubt, a cautionary flag rose when an outsider came in knowing the name of one of the sheltered children. Her attention shifted when the two kids with Janice started squabbling over who was going to brush the dog.

Carley nodded. Her eyes showed a minuscule bit of suspicion.

"I ran into Tara and her kids at the park the other day. She said to tell you that she loves you, and will see you soon."

Carley smiled.

"She's looking forward to your moving in with them," I said.

Overhearing my transgression into Carley's personal life, the houseparent turned toward us. Her accusatory frown was followed by, "It's time to do something else now."

I cringed.

God wanted me to continue the conversation. The four-year-old girl ran into the room screaming. The five-year-old boy followed, whacking her on the butt with a flyswatter. The housemother leaped toward them and took hold of the boy's arm while the girl escaped into the hallway.

"Time out!" She pointed to a single chair next to a tall bookcase. She marched the boy over to the chair. He sat, elbows on his knees, his face a sour pout cupped in his hands. The houseparent scolded him, reviewing rules and expectations. Returning to her desk, she held an eagle eye on the offending boy.

Carley spoke in a voice lower than the TV volume. "I hope I get to live with Aunt Tara and Uncle Ben. My father wants me to come live with him."

I hesitated. I did not know anything about her father. I defaulted to counselor-speak. "You would rather live with Tara and Ben than your father."

"Yes. He showed up out of nowhere. He isn't even my real father. I was adopted. I haven't seen him since I was a toddler and don't remember him at all. He walked out on mom and me. Grandpa and Ben were like my fathers. Then Grandpa died, then mom died, then I went to live with Grandma." Her face reflected the pain of her multiple losses.

"And she died too. Tara and Ben are your closest family."

"Yes, even my bio-mom gave me up at birth!" She bent over and wrapped her arm around Truman. He laid his head on her shoulder comforting her."

My heart broke for this girl. In the best circumstance, early teen years stunk. Throw in rejection and multiple tragedies, it's a formula leading to a serious meltdown.

"I love your dog," Carley said.

"Would you like us to come back next week?"

"I would like that. It will give me something to look forward to. If I'm still here, I can make some dog biscuits for Truman." She scratched his back and he wriggled under the touch of her fingers.

"He would like that."

A voice came from the dining area. "All hands on deck to set the table. Wash those hands first."

"I gotta go. Thanks for coming."

"You bet. It was great to meet you."

Soulman and Truman led the way out.

"Did you get to deliver your message?" Janice asked as we walked to our cars.

"Yes."

"Are you okay? You look shaken."

"I'll be alright. I leave therapy dog visits with one of two types of feelings. My job is to allow people to connect with my dog. I walk in knowing the people are hurting, emotionally, physically or both. I often leave feeling blessed that my dog cheered up people. Today was the other kind of visit. My dog brought comfort, but my heart broke and my soul aches."

"I understand. But when your heart aches, you still feel like you did the right thing. Right?"

"Intellectually, yes. Sometimes I wish I had an easier hobby," I said.

"You do what your personality dictates. Some folks golf, you and your dog like to bring comfort."

"I guess."

"You did good, girl. You gave Carley a gift."

I nodded. Truman peed on a tree, and we left.

Chapter 7

When I awoke the next morning, I checked the Peaceful Pets email and immediately regretted doing so.

Two emails from members showed the subject line, HELP! The theme from each member was the same. A former member, Ingrid, had contacted them and wanted her wheelchair returned. Her brother had surgery on his foot, and the doctor insisted he use a wheelchair. I noticed a third email from an address I did not recognize. It was from Ingrid, and like her, it was short and demanding. "Call me," followed by her phone number.

I deflated. The fact that she was a "former" member was a relief to all the current members. Whenever she opened her mouth, the purposes of her words were either to serve herself or to inflict pain on others. Exuding more energy than the average seventy-something woman, her mission in life appeared to be irritating those around her. I kept secret my wish for her internal battery to wear way down.

I debated calling her. Theoretically, handing over the wheelchair was simple, but my gut said Ingrid would manage to complicate the hand-over. Besides, I had no idea where I had stored it. I ended up with the thing four years ago when Peaceful Pets held our last training class at St. Bell's Church. I brought the wheelchair home with me to keep it from being assimilated into the church's paraphernalia. Then I moved to Jeanine and Rocky's place and the friends who helped me move loaded my storage shed with a mishmash of everything unimportant. The shed was organized by the rule of chaos.

Ingrid contacted me two years ago, asking for the wheelchair. With a lot of effort, I found it cleaned it up and called Ingrid three times but got no response. Two months later, Rocky offered to put it back in the shed. As far as I remembered, it was still there.

I loathed calling Ingrid, but since it was the right thing to do, I did. It would have been easier to do the wrong thing and not call.

"Hi, Ingrid, this is Margie Vonn. I understand you need your wheelchair, can you come pick it up?"

"Well, I guess. If that is what I must do."

Her tone crawled under my skin. "I will be glad to find it and clean it up, again. It's in storage."

"Why is it in storage? It shouldn't be in storage. What have you done with it?"

I held the phone away from my ear to protect my eardrum from her increased volume. *What was I supposed to do, keep it in my living room? This lady is a nutcase.*

"I have it in storage because you didn't pick it up two years ago when you said you wanted it."

"You could have brought it to me. You borrowed it. You should have returned it."

"I don't know where you live."

"You do too. You've been to my house."

"When have I ever been to your house?" *Lady, you are insane.*

"You could have called me, but you kept it. You should have given it back to me." Her voice morphed to screech level.

"Look, there is no reason to yell at me. You said you would pick it up two years ago, and you did not. So, I kept it for you. I should charge you a storage fee." *Yes! For pocket money, I could organize my shed and charge folks to store stuff.*

"Storage fee? You kept it. You took it. I should bring the sheriff with me."

I had enough. This lady had opened the gate and let my adrenaline out of its corral. I hung up the phone.

I stalked out to the shed to search for the stupid wheelchair. The appearance of the shed astonished me. I had forgotten that Rocky had volunteered to reorganize everything. In the last four years, I had only been through the first foot or two of the jumbled contents. The remaining six feet were uncharted territory.

The way Rocky had reorganized it I did not recognize anything. The wheelchair was AWOL. I flipped on the light and illuminated boxes, more boxes, cylindrical rolls I guessed were area rugs, and a dusty end table. Twenty minutes of digging did not reveal anything resembling a wheelchair. I wondered if I told Rocky to throw the rusty piece of junk in recycle or maybe donate it to a charity.

A car roared up the driveway and Truman sounded off with his threat bark. I hurried around to the front of my house. Over the top of the incoming car, I saw that the driver had not bothered to close the gate. The horses were in the front pasture with access to the open gate. I took off running as fast as my legs would go which was way slower than any horse.

As I passed the driver's side of the car, the window lowered and Ingrid stuck her head out.

"Don't you run from me!" She stuck her arm out and tried to grab me as I sprinted toward the gate.

If I did not get there before the equines noticed it was open, they would take off down the busy road. I was almost at the gate when Bitterroot lifted his head from grazing and oriented in the direction I ran.

A character as well as an escape artist, Bitterroot's miniature size allowed him to go where no horse had gone before. He ran for the open gate. The other grazing horses jerked up their heads. One by one they peeled away from the shrinking herd to gallop after Bitterroot. Ten hands tall, Bitterroot's legs were a blur. Snarky, Bitterroot's mini-buddy, challenged him for the lead racing like it was a truncated Kentucky Derby. The two full-sized horses followed the mini-pair bucking and cavorting, allowing their short-legged cousins to outdistance them.

"BACK!" I flailed my arms in the air.

Snarky checked his gallop by a couple miles per hour and fell back. The horses veered to the side and headed back the direction they came.

I arrived at the gate a half-length after Bitterroot exited. I slammed the gate shut, causing Snarky to slide to a halt, his ears pinned back. He spun, ran and ten feet away kicked out pretending he was kicking me. He took off running after the horses who knew better and were in rapid retreat. Bitterroot was the only escapee.

Devoid of his adoring heard, Bitterroot stopped and nibbled on the greener grass along the driveway. I squeezed through the gate and was glad the little urchin wore a halter.

"Here BB, come here. Nice pony." I headed toward him and heard Ingrid bang on the gate behind me.

"Here, take this." She held out a 12-inch carrot.

I wanted to grab the smaller end of the carrot and whack her in the head with it. I took it, and my better sense turned me around and instructed me to call the pony. Why on earth did she have a carrot, anyway?

"Come, BB, treat."

He ignored me. I took a baby step. He mirrored my motion and took a small step away toward the road. Ingrid, a second carrot in hand, made a wide berth around him and placed herself between the pony and the main road.

We played you-can't-catch-me for ten minutes. Riled up by Bitterroot's antics, the other horses whinnied and disappeared at a canter toward the barn. The fact that the others were gone may have contributed to Bitterroot's change of mind. He approached me and took the carrot. I took hold of his halter.

I hauled the pony through the gate, and he jerked the halter out of my hand. Ingrid slammed the gate shut. Bitterroot took off galloping toward the barn, tail up, nickering to his friends.

"Well at least you could thank me." Ingrid stood with her arms crossed, her face scowling.

I opened my mouth but restrained myself from uttering a word. What would come out would certainly be uncivil. I headed toward my house intent on distancing from the absurd woman. Ingrid stomped after me. I tried my best to ignore what she was saying. She caught up.

"Aren't you glad I brought carrots? I knew there were horses here, and I had this old bag that was starting to go bad."

Bad, limp carrots? Nope, they wouldn't work as clobbering tools. Can I find a thick stick? "I'm sorry, I haven't found the wheelchair yet. It doesn't seem to be in my shed." *Why was I sorry? Oh, because I had to talk to her.*

"You said you had it." She dropped her arms, hands fisted.

"I did have it, at some point, but I've had a lot of life changes in the last few years. I need some time to locate it."

"I don't have time! I need it now."

"I can't magically make it appear. If I could, I would." *Just to get rid of you.*

"Well! Call me as soon as you find it!"

She got in her car and threw gravel as she sped off. She did not bother to close the gate after her. I anticipated her carelessness and was already headed to the gate. I locked it, which was a rare phenomenon on this farm. I hoped Jeanine and Rocky had their keys. If not, their cars had horns. I would rather walk down and unlock the gate than face seeing that woman again.

I stewed in resentment juices for an hour then ate lunch. Either the adrenaline rush or time provided energy, that is if someone with Sjogrens ever had energy. I set off for my scheduled visit at Four Oaks without a clue of how the rest of the day would play out. I vowed to do this visit regardless of the unreasonable demands of Crazy Ingrid.

In the nursing home's foyer, I chatted with a family visiting their matriarch. The sound of the ancient Mrs. Shelton clomping her walker down the hall drew our attention. With each step Mrs. Shelton rocked back, intent on lifting her walker as high as she could. Due to her size and age it rose about an inch. As she rocked forward to step, she slammed the walker into the floor like a four-pronged jackhammer. For some not-so-odd reason, the screws on the walker were loose, so each step caused an auditory clump-rattle assault on nearby ears. Metallic noises unsettled Truman, so I put my hand on the side of his head to cover one ear and pressed his other ear against my thigh. He did not mind.

Mrs. Shelton slammed to a halt in front of me. Truman sat true. Experienced therapy dogs are desensitized to most off-the-wall human behaviors.

"I need an aide. Call me an aide!" Mrs. Shelton demanded.

You need a hearing aide. Tone it down a few decibels. "You need an aide?" I asked. I dropped back into the odd place between visitor and staff.

"Yes! Get me an aide!" Her eyes widening, her mouth pursed.

"Do you want me to have someone call Juan?" I suggested the only aide's name I could recall. It helped that I spied Juan down the hallway walking out of a room carrying a tray.

She upped her facial disgust to 'you total idiot' and yelled. "Yes! That's what I said. I only need one!"

Confused for a nano-second, I stifled a belly laugh then managed to sputter, "Okay."

The visit was off to an entertaining start. I walked to the nursing station and told a nurse Mrs. Shelton wanted an aide. Maybe Juan? Nursing homes produced unique, unintentional comedy. Visiting one regularly required a sense of humor.

I smiled at Juan as we passed in the hall. I did a double take back over my shoulder. Juan's skin was darker than any other Four Oaks aide. I guessed he was a mix of Hispanic and African heritage. He always dressed in charcoal gray, almost black scrubs. He made a dark picture, one that some would call black. Could he be The Black One, that Anna had referred to? I scribbled a note on my mental "to do" list. I needed to check out this Juan-guy. He appeared gentle and compassionate with the residents, but then so did Dr. Jekyll.

Truman and I made our rounds. We were the only team on duty, so we did not spend a lot of time with each resident. Lengthy therapy visits wore out Truman and me. My goal was to stay there for an hour.

"Hello, Mr. Smith." I approached mister eccentricity who was dressed in a lime green cycling shirt. "Are you going for a ride?"

"I would like to ride someone. Are you available?" He roared, amusing himself.

I tried to let it pass, understanding men from his generation thought women liked to be referred to as sex symbols. I was not apt to change him at this point in his life. I belonged to a different generation of thought.

"Not on your life. And I bet that if you did ride someone, you couldn't hold up to it and wouldn't have a life anymore. Are you headed for the goal posts Mr. I-know-when-someone-will-kick-the-bucket?"

Mr. Smith rocked back and forth. "Score! What a way to go!"

I shook my head and entered Anna's room. Covered up to her neck with blankets, her face resembled the end of a graying potato.

I pushed the wheelchair aside. "Hi, Anna. Truman is here for a visit. Do you want to pet him?"

She nodded.

I tapped the bed with my fingers. "Two paws," I said and Truman put his front paws on Anna's bed.

"Murder. Me next. I know," she mumbled and stroked Truman's paws. She sounded exhausted. I wondered how long it had been since she had slept through the night.

"You sound afraid."

"Yes. Black One. Me next. I know. Sad, so sad." She stroked Truman's paw. Her head dropped to the side and her eyes closed.

I watched to see if her cover rose with breaths. Satisfied she was still breathing, I pointed to the ground.

"Off, good dog," I whispered.

We left Anna's room and continued on our visit. We finished our third room-visit when I noticed a nice looking man entering Anna's room. I assumed he was her son.

I headed back to Anna's room to introduce myself, but an angry voice diverted my attention. The door to the nurse's break room stood ajar. I recognized Nurse Renee Blackwell's stressed voice. I stopped, leaned over and feigned tightening Truman's harness.

"But I don't have the money. It will kill him if I can't get it. Can you please give me a loan?"

Pause.

I assumed she was on the phone and was listening while the other person answered.

"Please! I don't know who else to ask." Her tone elevated.

Pause.

"I will do anything."

Lizzie Borden clomped down the hall in our direction. I re-fastened Truman's harness and caught a couple of his hairs in the clip. He scratched at the clip.

Borden stopped in front of me. "If that dog has fleas, get him out of here."

"Nurse Connelly, he does NOT have fleas. I was adjusting his harness," I countered.

Blackwell opened the door, turned away from us and hurried off.

Lizzie Borden brushed past me and entered the break room. She muttered under her breath. I caught the words, "volunteers, dogs, hmph."

I would have muttered the b-word back at her, but I liked female dogs.

I headed down the hallway, my benevolent spirit internally duking it out with my dislike of Lizzie Borden. Truman caught my eye. His eyes indicated he was concerned about me.

I rubbed Truman's neck with both hands, and the result was like a genie granting a wish for calming. Taking a deep breath, I let it out slowly, counting to four as I did. Remembering the man I assumed was Anna's son, I headed toward her room to introduce myself. I was almost there when the door opened and the man walked out. I smiled. He smiled back. He reminded me of Tom Cruise.

"Hi, I'm with Peaceful Pets. Is Anna your mother?"

He raised his eyebrows. "No, a friend." He reached down to pet Truman who had plopped on the floor. "Nice dog."

"Thanks," I said. *Nice man. I'd like you to visit me and my dog before I am a bedridden old lady.* What was with this lately, me and men?

"A pleasure to meet you. Sorry, I'm in a hurry," he said, then walked toward the exit.

I patted my thigh to get Truman up on his feet, and we continued down the hallway. It occurred to me we had not exchanged names. I hoped our paths would cross again.

Chapter 8

Leslie and I met for dinner at Olson's All-Day Breakfast Restaurant. I craved a cheddar-spinach omelet. It was one of those rare times when we were able to get together sans dogs. Once in a while, humans-only was in order.

In a symbolic gesture, we cleared the table between us. In place of the salt and pepper shakers and the blue vase holding a yellow silk flower, Leslie spread out an 11 x 18-inch sheet of paper. A myriad of numbered black dots filled the surface of the paper. She placed two pens, one red and one black in an empty cup beside the paper.

"It's been months since we've played, let's review the rules," Leslie said.

Leslie was always coming up with games whose purpose was to delve more deeply into life. I wasn't sure that is what I wanted to do at that moment. "If we must. I'm focused on food. I'm starving. You promise you don't know what the end picture is?"

"That's rule one. Of course, I don't know what it is. I picked it randomly."

"This beast must have over 200 dots. It looks like it might have palm trees, but I have no clue what that center mess is. This will take hours to finish connecting all the dots. I guess we don't have to finish it all in one night. We can save it for next time."

Leslie continued. "Rule 2. On your turn, you make a statement relevant to some issue currently bugging you. If you state a connection that is a fact, you draw a connecting line with a black pen. If you state an opinion, you draw the line with red pen."

"Rule 3. All the connections must somehow relate to the theme stated by the person drawing the first line," I said.

"And directly relate to the previous line's statement," Leslie said.

"When we are done, we can see if we are basing our conclusions more on facts or opinions. If there are more black lines, facts have driven the conclusion. If there are more red lines, our conclusions are opinion driven, and we need to dig up more facts. This is going to take forever."

"Your turn to go first. You can set the theme." Leslie pushed the cup holding the pens my way.

I chose the black one for a fact. "This morning when I called to schedule our next Four Oaks visit, Lizzie Borden told me that I was upsetting Anna."

Leslie picked up the red pen. "Lizzie was trying to make you feel guilty for engaging Anna in conversation."

I took the red pen. "Four Oaks does not like controversy."

"I'm not sure if that's an opinion or a fact," Leslie said.

"Meredith died." Leslie drew a black line.

"She may have been murdered." I drew a red line.

"Anna is not always coherent." Leslie's line was black.

I took the pens and put them down on the puzzle, our signal to stop and dig deeper.

"That was quick. She must have upset you," Leslie said.

"The whole thing is upsetting. Something is going on. The whole Black One thing is driving me nuts."

"The Black One? What are you talking about?"

"Remember? Anna said The Black One killed Meredith."

"Sure, I remember." Leslies eyes shot up to the ceiling.

I shook my head. "It probably doesn't make much difference, anyway. I've thought about it, and there are three possible suspects. Borden, AKA Nurse Connelly who is a black-hearted creep, Juan who looks black, and the head nurse Renee Blackwell whose name starts with 'black'."

"Why would any one of those people want to murder an old lady? Most of the residents at Four Oaks only live a few months or at most a couple of years before they die naturally. Why risk killing someone when a problem person would be dead soon, anyway?"

"I don't know. It would have to be someone mentally unstable and controlling, or sadistic."

Leslie squinted and picked up the red pen. "My Aunt Marnee befriended old folks at a retirement community where she worked. She targeted folks with no children, or estranged children. Aunt Marnee feigned dedicated care, love, compassion, whatever it took to get a dying person to sign over their estate to her. The truth is she took good care of them, better than any of their neglectful children did. Aunt Marnee would take them into her own home during the last few months of their lives. They usually died fairly soon after going to her house. She inherited several lucrative friend-inheritances for doing so. My family often tittered about whether or not Aunt Marnee helped matters along, so to speak. Ironically, Aunt Marnee's son sucked all the money she appropriated to feed his extravagant love life. Marnee died in a nursing home, broke and alone."

"See? It could be murder."

"I didn't say Aunt Marnee murdered them!"

I shot Leslie one of those, "ri-i-i-ght" looks.

"Was Meredith rich?" Leslie asked.

"I don't know. I only visited them. I don't think so. She shared a room, so I doubt it."

"Can we find out? Who could we ask?"

"We?" I asked.

"This sounds interesting. I want to be in on it. Let's check out the obits," Leslie suggested.

"Brilliant idea. What was Meredith's last name?" I pulled out my cell phone to search obituaries.

"Beats me. I guess I don't pay attention to folks' last names."

"We're a great pair of detectives. We're stuck on the first hurdle. Back to plan A. I'll talk to Four Oak's director. I'm scheduled to go back and visit soon."

"Plan A?"

"I always have plan A."

We finished our dinner without continuing our exercise of connect the dots.

———

Two days later, under the scrutiny of Sign-In-Sarah, I stopped to sign my name in the visitor log. Sarah was the gatekeeper at Four Oaks. No visitor got past Sarah. Years ago on my first visit, she demanded to see my driver's license and spent five minutes comparing the signature to what I put on the log. She demanded to see Truman's therapy dog credentials and compared the photo to his face.

"Hi, Sarah, how are you today?" I reached for the pen.

Sarah pointed to the blank line under the last signature. "Sign here."

"Would you like to pet my dog?" She never petted Truman but she liked to pet Rusta when Leslie came with me. I was solo today and felt I should be polite.

"No."

"No problem," I said and headed toward the director's office.

I peeked through the side glass and knocked on the door adorned with an oversized brass plate inscribed with Heather Hope Hillary. Ms. Hillary looked up, stood then checked her reflection in a compact mirror. On the way to the door, she smoothed the skirt of what I guessed was a navy Brooks suit. Her hair was pinned back in a tight twist.

She opened the door and I opened my mouth to speak, but Ms. Hillary beat me to it.

"Ah, one of our lovely therapy dog teams. The activity director is two doors down." She pointed and started to close her door.

"Wait, I'm here to see you," I said before the door shut all the way.

The woman's face glazed over. I expected her eyes to roll, but they did not.

"I see. What can I help you with?"

"It's rather private."

Ms. Hillary drew in a breath and huffed it out her nose. "I've got a minute." She pulled the door open, turned her back to me and returned to her desk. Truman and I scooted in, and I shut the door behind us. The starkness of the cool gray walls, bright white trim and black furniture was interrupted by two original Disney cartoon cels, one of Pluto and one of Goofy.

"I like your Disney cels." Without waiting for an invitation, I sat in one of the chairs in front of her desk.

"Thank you."

"I'm Margie Vonn and this is Truman."

"Heather Hillary, Director." Her hands remained folded on her desk. She could have been a model for a business-Barbie doll.

"How are you doing today?" I stalled to organize my strategy. It occurred to me that I should have developed a strategy before I knocked on her door.

"Fine."

"I have a concern about one of your patients." I debated whether that was too blunt.

"They are residents. This is not a hospital. Which resident?"

"Meredith, Anna's roommate."

"Meredith Marshall?"

"I'm not sure of her last name, but they were roommates until Meredith died."

"What is your concern?"

"Anna keeps telling me that Meredith was murdered."

"That is not an unusual statement from residents who fear death and feel it is unnatural."

I vowed not to cave. "Okay, then let me explain my concerns. Anna keeps accusing someone she refers to as The Black One."

"And who do you think The Black One might be?" Her tone sounded like a tired parent indulging a young child afraid of monsters under the bed.

"I don't know for sure, and I don't want to accuse anyone specific."

Ms. Hillary glared at me over the top of her designer glasses.

"There are a few staff members it could be, but I came here to call your attention to Anna's accusations," I said.

"Let me guess." Without raising her hand off the desk, she pointed toward the glass panel next to the door.

I turned at the precise moment Lizzie Borden stomped by.

"Would Nurse Connelly be your suspect?" She asked, inclining her head toward Lizzie.

"I'm not sure, but maybe."

"Nurse Connelly cares more for the residents than any other nurse I have ever seen. She is my most competent nurse. Her rough exterior compensates for a soft and compassionate heart. Don't you dare consider implicating her in a foul scheme."

"There are more. Like Renee Blackwell. She's stressed and is having some sort of financial issues. The part of her name 'Black' could indicate that's who Anna was talking about. Then there's the dark skinned Juan who always wears dark scrubs. Anna might be saying Black Juan."

Ms. Hillary sat for a second. I hoped I had made some headway. She took a slow deep breath.

"Ms. Vonn. I appreciate your concern. I don't mean to be caustic, but over the years I have seen many volunteers who have been overly concerned about the personal lives of our residents or staff. It is my understanding that your volunteer position description does not include evaluating our people.

"We do appreciate your therapy dog teams. They cheer up our residents and stimulate their social and mental interactions. But please leave staff and resident evaluations to us. I'm very protective of both my residents and my staff. I do not want to hear speculation. If you have something concrete then please bring it to my attention. Otherwise, please continue on with your job of bringing joy and comfort." She stood up, walked to the door and opened it.

"Do me one favor," I said as I got up.

"What's that?"

"Ms. Hillary, please have someone you trust go talk to Anna. Ask her about The Black One."

"Your discourse indicates that you are not aware that Dr. Anna Longmire passed away two days ago. I believe it was same day as your last visit." Her manicured nails tapped on the doorframe.

I caved. I failed in my first attempt at investigation. Everything was wrong. Anna was dead. My gut told me something was up, but I had no solid connections. Was Ms. Hilary in on it? I knew I had a lot to learn. I headed toward the door.

The eccentric Mr. Smith had said he had the ability to predict natural deaths, so I asked one last question. "What about Mr. Perkins, did he pass, too?" I wanted to confirm that Mr. Smith had a sixth sense for the death angel's timing.

Ms. Hillary tucked her chin. "Yes, the same night as Dr. Longmire. Death is one of the ongoing sorrows of Four Oaks. We never get used to it. Ms. Vonn, I can see you deeply care for our people and death upsets you. Try to remember that with few exceptions, all these people here are at the ends of their lives. Death is a common occurrence here. Death is part of the natural process of life. In some cases, death is a huge relief. We try to keep our residents comfortable until the inevitable. Death is inevitable for us all. Ultimately, none of us can stop it."

My skin responded by erupting into a fleeting case of goose bumps. In my opinions, Ms. Hillary was too comfortable with death.

Chapter 9

A cool breeze flowed across my face as I walked from my car to the doors of the Water Tree Public Library. Inside, the temperature rose with each step as I trudged upstairs to the meeting room. Thirty-five people sat on folding chairs waiting for the Peaceful Pets meeting to start. Fifteen newbies thumbed through our group's introductory handouts. No dogs graced the room, as only service dogs were allowed in the library. Truman doubled as a mobility service dog when I needed him, but his dual career muddied the waters at therapy dog meetings so I left him at home.

Our handouts explained the restriction, pointing out that our therapy dogs were not service dogs but rather dogs that provided therapy to others. Sometimes unscrupulous therapy dog owners tried to pass off their well-behaved dogs as service dogs. That severe offense resulted in forfeiture of membership. Before the meeting started, the brochures helped weed out folks who thought that registering their dog as a therapy dog would allow them to take their pet into stores or on public transportation.

LouLou called the meeting to order. Meetings were short and sweet so our members and legitimate new folks would not regret attending. We did our business, old and new, and adjourned.

"Anyone interested in socializing please join us at Healthy Homestead Eats," I announced. Sixteen people walked to the restaurant two doors down.

Healthy Homestead offered a variety of meals from contemporary to southern comfort food. Glossy pine walls and chunky wood furniture adorned the interior. Retro aluminum chairs surrounded tables covered with course linen cloths. The festive vinyl chair seat pads were all the colors of the rainbow. Traditionally, the service was great. This evening our server was the sassy Anita.

She took our orders and when the food was ready, she expertly set our meals in front of each person without needing to ask whose plate was whose. It took three trips and a helper to serve us all. When Anita completed her task, she stood at the head of the table and spread her fingers out pointing them toward her temples. She stretched her eyes wide and in a spooky voice said, "From your personal demeanor, I bet I can guess the description of each of your dogs."

LouLou challenged her. "Two bucks for each one you can guess. Dog owner pays."

The group agreed. The waitress was on.

She pointed to LouLou. "Yours is small. Black and White. Long hair. A Shih Tzu, maybe?"

Giggles spread through the group and LouLou pulled two dollars from her purse. "Shih Tzu mix, but close enough."

Anita circled the table addressing each member of the group. Ten of her sixteen guesses were correct. We shook our heads, dumbfounded.

"Have you been looking at our photos?" LouLou asked.

Anita shook her head.

"How do you do it?" Janice asked.

Smiling, Anita put her hands on her hips. "Easy. I can tell the dogs' color and hair length from the hair on your jackets and shirts."

Everyone examined their sleeves and picked off dog hairs.

"But how could you tell if they were large or small?" LouLou asked.

"If you have more dog hair on the front of your clothes and sleeves, you've probably been holding your dog in your arms. Folks with big dogs have more hair on their legs and the backs of their clothes because they only clean off their fronts."

"You need to get a private investigator license," LouLou said.

We twittered and picked hair off each other like a bunch of monkeys. Each person, including the folks she missed, threw in two bucks.

"She is a hoot," Leslie said.

Janice, Judith and I were sitting at the end of the long table with Leslie, and we all agreed.

Although Charlotte's toy poodle Inky was not a therapy dog, she made it a habit to attend all the dog group meetings in town. I was glad she was at the other end of the table with a few of her groupies, and that I remained out of her conversations.

"Let me tell you about my last visit to Four Oaks. Be forewarned," I said, my voice low.

"Tell us," Janice encouraged.

"Mr. Smith—"

"Sexual harassment?" Janice jumped in.

"Bingo. You knew! He's a hoot," I said.

"I don't know how men of that generation could think we like to be objectified," Leslie said.

"Movies. People take fiction for reality," Judith said, clicking her thumbnail against the nail of her middle finger. "In the past, people thought what they saw on the big screen represented the way people were supposed to behave."

"Sometimes fiction is close to reality," Leslie said.

"And sometimes reality is stranger," Judith said.

"I would like to live in Star Wars." I made a motion over my head pretending I wielded a light saber.

"Good versus evil has been reality since the beginning of time. You can't always tell who is who," Judith said.

"Like the Garden of Eden," Leslie said.

"So is it fact or fiction that Meredith was murdered? What do you think?" Judith said.

Leslie drew back in her chair, crossed her arms and huffed out audibly. "Plausible, but not likely."

"I think Anna was telling the truth and someone killed Meredith," I said.

"Why?" Judith asked.

"That's the problem," I said. "I can't think of a motive. Anna was so insistent. I don't think it was a delusion. She stuck hard with what she believed."

Charlotte's voice hailed from the far end of the table. "Judith, come join us down here. We are talking Hound Dog Pawty and we need your no-nonsense money skills."

"Excuse me, ladies, I'm being called." Judith moved to the group at the far end of the table.

"I have an idea for a possible motive," Janice said.

Leslie and I whipped our heads toward Janice.

"What?" We said.

"You know that Meredith was Ben Marshall's mother, right?"

"Tara's husband?" I asked.

"Right," Janice said.

"What is your point? Did he murder his mother? I'm not sure who he is," Leslie said.

"We talked to his wife, Tara, and their kids at the park one day. They were on the playground. Carley's uncle," I said.

"The two ladies with all the little kids?"

"Yes. The other day, I was pulling weeds at the park and I heard a couple of men arguing. Being my curious self-"

"Nosy," I teased.

Janice grimaced. "Curious. I peeked through the bushes to see who it was. Ben was arguing with that Wentworth guy."

"Wentworth guy?"

"He has been walking his dogs in the park a lot recently. I'm surprised you haven't seen him."

"And?" Leslie put both palms on the table and leaned forward.

"And they were too far away to hear everything, but they were arguing something about custody of Carley. Wentworth was claiming Carley was his daughter and he wanted to get her back. He said he was young and dumb when he left her. He wanted to be her father now."

"Carley? Tara's Carley?" I asked.

"Yes, right. Ben is married to Tara. Ben is Carley's adoptive uncle. Wentworth was married to Carley's mother ages ago," Janice said.

"How do you know all this?" I asked.

"I go to the same church as Tara and Ben."

"Go on," I said.

"Ben told Wentworth he has been her functional father and he wanted to adopt her. He said the Marshalls were her family. Carley's last name proves that is what Olivia wanted."

"Olivia?" I asked.

"Carley's adoptive mother, Ben's sister. When Olivia divorced Wentworth, she took back her family name. She got full custody of Carley and changed their last names from Wentworth to Marshall."

"And Olivia died?" Leslie asked.

"Yes. Cancer. It was sad, but Meredith took in Carley and did a great job raising her."

"Poor Carley, then her adoptive grandmother died at Four Oaks," I said.

Janice nodded. "I was surprised when Meredith died. Soulman and I had visited her the day before and she seemed so much better. She was talking about going home the next week."

"And?" I prompted.

"That's all I have. That's it." Janice said.

"That's it?" Leslie asked. "An argument? We knew legal issues hampered Carley's custody. Tara mentioned that. It's true that there is a connection between Wentworth and Meredith. What's Wentworth's first name?"

"Brain hiccup. I can't remember," Janice said twisting her lips.

"So who would need to murder Meredith and for what reason?" I said.

"It could have been Ben, if Meredith was going to sign custody over to Wentworth. Ben was angry," Janice said.

"Ben murdering Meredith to get custody? If Ben was a murderer, he would likely murder Wentworth, not Meredith."

"Good point," Janice said.

"The Marshalls put their hearts into raising the girl. The Marshalls are not blood-kin, but they were legal family through the court. It isn't likely they would give Carley's estranged stepfather anything but visitation rights. We are missing something. We don't have a legit motive. Heck, we don't even have a suspect," Leslie said.

"I suspect The Black One, whoever that is," I said.

Janice snapped her dark-skinned face toward me.

"That's what Anna said, not me," I said.

Our group finished their meals and shuffled through the game of social-seat-switch, allowing opportunities to chat with everyone. Eventually, people said their goodbyes and headed home one at a time. Leslie and I were the only ones left sipping decaf.

"So back to The Black One's motive. If we can figure out who has a motive, we may have the killer," Leslie said.

"You sound like you might be convinced there was a murder."

"It's exciting to think about it."

"I'm only brain storming, not accusing, but nurse Renee Blackwell desperately needs money. It's just a guess but Anna may have suspected Renee Blackwell was trying to squeeze money from Meredith. And there's Juan who looks black."

Leslie's face morphed into a bewildered frown.

"What? It's true."

"Anyone else? Anyone at all?" Leslie asked.

"I went to the office of the Four Oaks director. Ms. Hillary's office furniture is all gray and black. Rather cold and austere. Heartless. The only bits of cheer in the whole room are a couple of original Disney cels."

"Mr. Smith is the Disney nut, not Anna or Meredith."

"I know, but Ms. Hillary has an attitude. It's like she thinks she is in control of the world. Neither Anna nor Meredith were the richest residents.

One of the residents told me that the woman who moved into Meredith and Anna's room has a ton of money. She has the room to herself. Single rooms are expensive. One less resident to care for reduces stress on the staff. If they treat her well, she'll give positive references which may attract the old lady's peers. More money, less work. Every CEO's dream. Maybe Ms. Hillary hurried the process," I said.

"We are still missing something. What is it?"

"How do you figure out what you don't know?"

"We think about it."

I avoided Leslie's eyes. My worst fear was of what I did not know.

We left it at that.

Chapter 10

Bright morning air invited Truman and me for a long walk. The pastures sparkled with buckets of dew and would soak Truman the minute he stepped off the gravel farm road. I did not feel like dealing with a wet dog, so I loaded him up and drove to Bullard Park where the trails were landscaped and dry.

Truman hopped out of the car, eager to explore. This humid morning, even the trail mulch glistened and wafted a moist organic odor but only his paws would get wet.

We headed straight for the trail that led through the woods. I stopped to focus my binoculars on a high-pitched tweeting from the trees. Hot on a super-scent, Truman yanked on the leash pulling the binoculars off my face. I capitulated and walked on. Sometimes he needed to have the privilege to be a dog. There would be plenty of birds for me to observe down the trail.

Nose to the ground and tail a "c" over his back, Truman zigzagged across the trail, catching the leftover scents of last night and the fresh ones from early morning. Like most dogs, Truman's superpower was seeing with his nose. I wondered if dogs mapped the smells linearly, chronologically, or more like a scatter graph. The alternative was they mind mapped in a manner that humans never imagined.

The forest displayed its transitioning from spring green to summer green. The leaves were almost full. The understory popped colors of marvelous spring wildflowers. We came to a grouping of mayapples. They reminded me of fancy gnome umbrellas, especially the single stemmed male plants. Except for one early bloomer, the flower buds on the y-stemmed female plants were tight. A grouping of maroon wake-robin trillium hung on in the shade. I recalled a description of these unobtrusive forest plants, "Flowers solitary, arising stemless from a whorl of leaves." Each flower reminded me of a burgundy phoenix rising from a green tri-lobed podium.

The miniature jackhammer sound and chirps of a red-bellied woodpecker punctuated the air. I spied it through my binoculars. The red streak starting at its beak and running over the crown to the shoulders pegged it as a male. It flew off as we approached.

Sharp chirping scolded me from above but I could not locate the bird making the noise, likely a LBB—little brown bird—of some sort. Noisy bird-song harmonies radiated from the treetops. I hoped none decided to do concerto number 2 on my head. Close to where the trail neared the edge of the woods, cedar waxwings flitted around a small-leafed tree searching for insects. We neared the lake, and a near-by night heron's call sounded off like a squeaky-toy. Not fooled by the bird, Truman ignored it.

Truman halted and I bumped into his rear end. He alerted toward the bushes at the left of the trail. Thick privet, that destructive, invasive, horrible shrub, blocked the view of whatever caught his attention.

"Is it a deer? Stay," I whispered, and pulled out my phone to snap a photo. I crept up to where Truman stood and followed his stare. I located the object of interest, the back of a man in a tan ball cap standing close to an ancient oak tree. His arms were in front of him and he was looking downward. He gave a little shake then started to turn around, and I realized what he had been doing.

"Oops," I whispered to Truman and tugged him down the trail.

We had made it ten feet down the trail, when a high-pitched barking erupted behind us. Truman and I swung around.

A tan and white corgi challenged our presence. On the other end of the leash, was a man in a ball cap and sunglasses. He looked like the man who I assumed was Anna's son.

"Hello." I held Truman back from the yapping corgi.

"Hi. Sorry about my yapper. I hope he didn't scare you." The man reached down and picked up the dog. It stopped barking.

"Cute corgi." Truman was beyond the corgi's reach, and had never been aggressive. I was not worried about him, but the corgi's intentions were not clear.

"I'm Paul." He walked forward and held out his hand for an introductory handshake.

"Margie," I said, shaking his hand.

"Nice to meet you. Beautiful morning for a walk, isn't it?"

"Didn't I see you visiting someone at Four Oaks Nursing and Rehab a few days back?"

Paul's eyebrows raised above his sunglasses, and his mouth opened for an instant. He closed it and smiled. "Sorry, no. You must have seen one of my many doppelgangers."

Face recognition was not one of my strong points.

"I'm headed toward the playground. Do you want to walk with me?" he asked.

"Sure."

He put the corgi down and inadvertently dropped the leash. The rude beast leaped forward and latched on to Truman's foreleg. Truman screeched. Paul reached down and grabbed his dog and the corgi let go. A small hole in Truman's leg oozed blood.

"I'm so sorry. This little urchin is a mess."

Sarcasm kicked in. *I'd like to mess with him, the horrid little rat.* Keeping my thoughts to myself, I bent down to examine my dog's leg.

"It looks like he needs treatment or at least a good sterile cleaning. If you want to take him to the vet, I will gladly pay the bill. Let me know how much," Paul said.

"I'll take him to Jerry Elliston. You can check with him later to pay the bill." I was not in the mood to exchange contact information, or to thank the man.

I stomped off and Truman followed, checking behind him with his tail half tucked.

Pulling into the driveway of the animal clinic, I saw Jerry walking out the side door toward his car. I pulled up and rolled down the window.

"Hi. It's a pleasure to see you. I have the afternoon off and I'm heading to Can-Con to pick up some food and grab a cup of coffee. Do you want to join me?" Jerry asked.

"Truman has an injury. He needs his leg examined and cleaned. Some idiot little dog grabbed his leg and chomped a nice hole in it. Is Lynn here?"

"Go on in the side door. I'll doctor it, but only if you'll have coffee with me afterward," Jerry said.

"Sounds like a deal to me."

Truman was not limping, so I knew the wound was not deep. Home treatment would have been adequate, but as long as that idiot corgi's owner was paying, I chose to have an expert treat it. I led Truman onto the lift table and slung my arm around him for security. Jerry raised the table and examined the laceration.

"Not bad. I'll clean the wound and apply antibiotic cream. It bled enough to help clean itself out. Was the dog wearing a rabies tag?

I nodded. "He appeared plenty healthy and well cared for, but he was an uncontrolled brat."

"Like Ginger? Poor Truman has been getting pummeled by the little guys lately."

"True! I hope he doesn't decide to fight back some day. He's big enough to do some damage."

"He's too much of a gentleman," Jerry said. He finished cleaning the wound and ruffled Truman's neck. "Such a good boy you are."

The small wound did not require bandaging, but Jerry wrapped it anyway.

"How much did all this cost?"

"It's on me. You can pay for the coffee this time."

"Oh, no. The brat-dog's owner said he would pay, and I want him to pay. Bill me the usual charge for this visit. He said he would come by and pay the bill later." I paused, "On second thought, why don't you charge double your normal fees."

Jerry cracked a smile. "It's not a bad idea to teach a lesson, but it's not ethical."

We drove our cars to Can-Con. I ordered two coffees while Jerry and Truman waited at a table.

The lid on the cup prevented a hot mess when I tripped over my own feet.

"Easy now, girl." Jerry smiled and cocked his head.

Men calling women girls normally irritated me, but he sounded more like he was soothing a nervous horse than repudiating my social status. I tried to relax but my nerves crackled. His adorable head cock was getting to me.

Was this a date? Leslie would surely ask. What difference would it make whether it was a date or coffee with a friend? I stiffened, flashing back to the oppressive relationship with my deceased husband. I shook off the thoughts. This man wanted to enjoy coffee and conversation. He did not want to control me. I drew in a deep breath and released it slowly.

Jerry updated me on some of Ginger's latest antics, and I told him about baby goat yoga. A comfortable pause allowed me to compose myself. Charlotte's squeaky voice bursting out from behind me decomposed the tranquility.

"Dr. E! Margie! I'm so glad to see you."

At first, I did not see her marauding pee-body dog. I located him peering out of an over-the-shoulder dog carrier, his nose pressed against the screen.

"Let me grab myself a coffee, and I'll join you." Charlotte did not give us a chance to respond, not that either of us was cruel enough to deny her.

I relaxed when Charlotte put Inky's carrier on the floor with the dog still inside. At least I did not have to worry about the little dog lifting its leg on Truman.

"So what are you two up to?" Charlotte chirped.

Nice way to embarrass us, and it's none of your business.

"How's planning for the Howling event going?" Jerry asked.

I was grateful he redirected the conversation.

"Oh, wonderful! Everything is on target. It will be so much fun."

"Have you gotten enough donations to cover all the expenses?" I asked.

"Yes, they are steadily coming in. I've received pledges for a little over the amount I predicted we would need. I'm glad for the buffer. You know how things always run over."

A woman walked close behind me. She reached the register and placed a super-size can of goldfish flakes on the counter then dug in her purse. My mind gyrated then landed on positive ID. It was Tara. She saw me and waved. The clerk turned to prep her coffee and Tara walked over to our table.

"Charlotte, Dr. E, Margie, good to see you," she said.

"You too. Would you like to join us?" I asked.

"Thanks, but I have to pick up the little ones. I need to run. I wanted to say hi and thank you for visiting Carley."

"I was happy to do it. I hope things are moving forward for you."

"Yes, I think everything is going okay."

The clerk called Tara back to the counter to pick up her coffee.

"Gotta run." Tara waved. She picked up her coffee and fish food and headed to the front of the store.

"You know about Carley?" Charlotte asked. Without waiting for an answer, she launched into babble mode. "I hope Tara gets custody. The girl's adoptive father is a louse. Did you know the new Peaceful Pets lady with the corgi...what's her name?"

"Judith," I barely got the word in before Charlotte gushed on.

"She knows him. Oh, never mind. Rumor has it that Carley is inheriting a bit of a bundle. It would pay off the louse's debts and take care of any other money issues. I bet that's the real reason he's trying to get custody."

Jerry's eyes rolled, and he rubbed his forehead with two fingers as if he was pressing Charlotte's words from his head.

"Excuse me, please." He headed to the men's room.

My mind spun. Thoughts bumped between paying attention to Charlotte and trying to connect the dots between Meredith's death and money. I had no solid connection. This was the first time I knew of a possible money motive, if in fact what Charlotte referred to as a bundle, was actually a lot of money.

"That creep left them high and dry when Carley was a baby, and now, poof, he shows up and says he wants to care for her," Charlotte said. "I don't buy it. He doesn't want to be a father. It's obvious there is something more."

"Is his name Wentworth?" My mind spun, remembering what Janice had said about someone named Wentworth arguing with Carley's uncle Ben Marshal.

"Yes," Charlotte replied.

Charlotte's watch beeped. "Oh, no! I forgot about my hair appointment. I have got to run!" She picked up her coffee, grabbed Inky's carrier and scurried away.

I glanced toward the men's room. Jerry stuck his head out from behind the door and mouthed the words, "Is it safe?"

I nodded and he rejoined me at the table.

"Chicken," I teased.

"Bwak!" Jerry stuck his fists in his armpits and flapped mock wings.

'Truly." I shook my head.

"What was that all about?" Jerry asked.

"Beats me." I had to think a minute before I confided in Jerry and divulged my suspicions. I did not know him well enough to share secrets.

"Charlotte is a crack-up," Jerry commented.

"I guess you could call her that. Who needs a town paper when you've got Charlotte?"

"Seriously, what was she talking about?" Jerry asked again.

I took a chance and decided to share my nursing home concerns with Jerry. I explained why I was suspicious of Meredith and Anna's deaths.

"Money is a favorite motive for murder. But unless there is an urgent need and a lot of money, it's not likely someone would take the chance and murder an old person destined to die soon. Do you think this adoptive father might be a suspect?" Jerry asked.

"I have no evidence. Up until now, there was not an iota of a motive for murder. I'll ask Judith about this guy. Tara never said anything about Carley's getting an inheritance. How can I convert rumor to fact?"

"Can we have dinner tonight? We can talk about it if you want." His head did that endearing tilt thing.

I envisioned him as an inquiring beagle puppy. I had to stop that.

"Dinner? I hate to leave Truman by himself. I don't want him to bother his wound." I reached down and scratched the dog's back.

"Typical worried, dog mom. I wasn't asking you to go out. I know Truman's health is important to you. Tell me what you want and I'll pick up groceries, bring food to your place and cook it for you. I'm an expert griller, if you like grilled. Whatever you want. Let me know. Cooking is my hobby." He patted his belly.

"Sure." A prickle of anxiety rolled like a tumbleweed down my spine. This man exuded kindness and compassion. That scared me.

I sought safety in blathering on about Rocky and Jeanine's critters. As my mouth shared stories, my brain searched for neutral directions to lead the conversation when I ran out of goat and DonQui tales.

Jerry's phone text dinged. He read it and grimaced. "Lynn needs help with a Great Dane having stomach issues. So much for the afternoon off. It should only take a couple of hours at most. Text me what you want me to bring for dinner and your address. I'll run by the store and then to your place as soon as I'm done at the clinic." He stood.

I sensed he wanted to say something else, but he turned and left.

I gulped the sugary dregs of my lukewarm coffee, and headed home.

Jerry arrived at my house at 4:30. At my request, he grilled split Cornish game hens and veggies, all locally sourced.

I was a little nervous. I suspected this was a date, even though we were not going out anywhere. I wondered how the night would end. If we had gone out, I could always excuse myself and go home. Here, I was stuck. We sipped wine while we waited for the hens to crisp brown.

"Growing up, what family dog was your favorite?" I asked, engaging in safe but somewhat relevant conversation. This guy seemed considerate, but I was not ready to trust his intentions. I did not want a close relationship, yet. I still felt the burning pain from memories of my ex.

"We had a black and tan, Pembroke Corgi, named Queeny. When I was ten, she was my soul mate, a sweet dog with enough of a mischievous personality to keep us entertained. One day, she got into the laundry basket and pulled out all my older sister's underwear and hauled them outside through the doggie door. There were bras and panties all over the yard. My sister almost died from embarrassment. Of course, her boyfriend was visiting and we were both in stitches. I helped clean up the yard and as my sister reached for the last pair of panties, Queeny swooped in, snatched the prize and engaged in a 5-minute game of keep away. The boyfriend almost fell down the deck stairs laughing. My sister dumped the poor guy after that."

"At least she left him with a hysterical story," I said.

"True."

"Peaceful Pets has a new lady with a corgi. She wants to do therapy dog work. She's a new banker in town, Judith Kimble. She finished her second observation visit the other day. She's starting her supervised visits with her dog."

"Gonzo?"

"You know them?"

"Yes. Gonzo is a sweet dog. I think he'll be fine at therapy work. He's a little young, but he'll settle down a bit."

"From what I've heard, I think he'll be good too. I hope Judith sticks with it," I said.

"He's a cute wiggle butt."

I liked the way this man talked, which made me more nervous. He seemed to be enjoying my company. He was comfortable, low key, no pressure and easy to talk to. Although not a Chris Hemsworth look-a-like, he was genuine.

A slight frown shadowed Jerry's face. I braved myself and asked, "Your face says something is bothering you."

"I was thinking about that corgi breeder Judith got her dog from. Sometimes I wonder about how Paul treats his dogs."

"Paul?" I startled at the name. "That was the name of the man whose corgi bit Truman."

"You didn't say a corgi bit him."

"You didn't ask, and I didn't think the breed was important. That's that guy Judith got Gonzo from?"

"Yes. I'm sure she paid a bundle for that pooch. Wentworth's corgis are not cheap."

"Wentworth? Paul...Wentworth?" I choked.

"Yes, is that a problem?"

"Do you know anything about his history?"

"I'm new in town," Jerry said. "I'm only familiar with his dogs."

I did not intentionally push the throttle to high, but my rampaging thoughts concocted a surprising conclusion. I needed to talk to Charlotte. She would have the scoop on Paul Wentworth.

I reset realistic priorities to revisit later. Right now, I intended to relish my dinner with Jerry.

Chapter 11

Drippy clouds sprinkled on Truman and me as we walked up the sidewalk to Four Oaks. I wiped the moisture off the dog and headed to the activity room.

"Get the doctor!" A high-pitched thready voice got the attention of everyone within earshot.

A man was slumped sideways over the arm of his wheelchair, and an aide ran over and knelt beside him. A second aide ran into the room followed by a rotund doctor puffing like an overloaded train.

I watched with the other residents. The doctor and the aide stretched the man out on the floor, and the doctor listened for breaths and heart sounds.

"Sorry, he's gone," the doctor said to the semi-circle of residents who had gathered.

"Don't say that! Do something," screeched the lady who had called for help.

"He has a DNR," the doctor said. "It was his time."

The aides started clearing the activity room, so I moved on.

A bit disconcerted, I passed Mr. Smith's room. Truman stopped by the door, eager to visit. He liked Mr. Smith. I knew he and his Disney collection would take my mind off the resident dying. Mr. Smith's door was closed, and a nurse's cart was sitting beside it. I rarely knock on doors because, if they are closed there is a reason. This door was pushed to the jamb but not tight enough to engage the latch. While I debated whether this meant the door was open or closed, Truman nosed the door open.

Nurse Renee Blackwell's eyes widened and Mr. Smith squinted. Renee was sitting on the edge of the bed, and Mr. Smith was lying on his back under the covers. Renee jerked her hand out from under the covers, rolled Mr. Smith to his side and straighten the covers around him.

"I'm so sorry, Truman pushed the door open."

"Bring him in." Mr. Smith waved his arm inviting us in. "I would love to see you."

Renee left the room.

I was not sure what was going on between Mr. Smith and Renee. I was not sure I wanted to know if it was anything more than straightening the covers.

"Your Disney collection always cheers me up. I love it," I said.

"You and your dog cheer ME up. Come here, Truman." Mr. Smith patted the bedspread, and Truman put the front half of his body on the bed. His hind feet stayed on the floor. Mr. Smith ruffled Truman's ears and scratched his neck.

"I have a hodgepodge of Disney collectables. Some are near worthless. Some are highly sought after. My son Josh said when I croak, he's going to sell the good ones, and give away the junk," Mr. Smith said.

"That's harsh."

"He says it much more politely than that, but that's what it boils down to. If you see anything you like, tell me. Josh knows that a lot of the pieces have names taped on the backs or bottoms. Those pieces are already claimed. Josh isn't hurting for money and it's more work for him to sell this stuff than to give a piece away. He'll be glad to give them to the folks whose names are on them."

"Thank you. That is very kind of you." My eyes wandered to the cels on the walls.

Mr. Smith followed my eye. "You like the cels? Some of them aren't worth much and Josh won't want them. Put your name on the back. I keep painter tape and a marker in the drawer there. Go ahead and pick one out."

"Can I pick something on my next visit?" It felt weird to put something on lay-away, waiting for the owner to die.

"You never know, I may not be here tomorrow."

"You look plenty healthy to me."

Mr. Smith flashed his dentures. "I should last awhile, but I'm tired of seeing folks around me drop like flies. I've been here for two years, and I lost count of who has died. I have to read the names on the doors to reckon if someone is still alive."

I hated when conversations deteriorated to how long residents had left to live. I could be run over by a semi-truck on the way home. My theory was to do my best to make the most out of life each day. Period. I hated when people added, 'while you can,' at the end of that statement.

"Go on, pick one, any one. Do it now. It will make this old man happy. Take a production cel for Truman. Put his name on the back. He's half of your cheer-up team. He deserves something."

"I'm not sure which one he would like." I grinned and scanned the cels, delaying my answer.

"Then get something for yourself."

I noticed a small 101 Dalmatians Christmas sleigh driven by Pongo and Perdita. The sleigh carried a snow globe containing Dalmatian puppies. It was one of those fast food Christmas promotional toys.

When I was six, for Christmas my babysitter gave me a similar sleigh that she had gotten when the 1966 movie came out. It was a hand-me-down, but I did not care. I loved the Dalmatians, but I think what I liked most was that every time I shook it, the snow fell somewhere new.

My plain snow globe was not as kitschy as this one which had sparkling rhinestones imitating snow all along the sleigh's runners. Golden glitter twinkled inside the globe. Tiny red and green glassy stones decorated Pongo's and Perdita's collars. I preferred rustic and natural, so the sleigh was not my style, but it was dogs and a connection to my youth.

"This one looks good." I said pointing to the snow globe. "I used to have one like it but lost it. Every Christmas I hope it turns up. Mine wasn't so sparkly. I loved the Dalmatians movies. I've seen them all at least 10 times."

Mr. Smith grinned. "Are you sure? There are plenty more that are bigger and flashier."

"This one is flashy enough. I like the dogs."

"Put your name on the bottom of it. Don't lose that one. You can always remember me every Christmas."

"Stop, you're breaking my heart."

Mr. Smith tapped his hand on his chest. "I'm glad I can still break a girl's heart."

I left Mr. Smith smiling. The Margie/Truman team visit was a success.

Nurse Renee came out of a room down the hallway. As I walked by, she stepped in front of me and touched my arm.

"Don't judge me," she said.

"I assume you're talking about Mr. Smith."

"The man has needs. He is kind, and he knows he won't be here long. I can provide him what he needs."

Sarcasm brain jumped into all sorts of sordid scenarios. I harnessed the thoughts before I said something off color and rude. I was embarrassed, too. I said the only thing I could think to say, "That is kind of you."

Renee locked her eyes on mine. "Look, I don't do it for free. He is a generous and appreciative old man. I need the money. It's a long story and no fault of my own."

I wondered if this service was unique to Four Oaks or common in all places like this. I had absolutely no idea.

"And don't even think about reporting me. Have you seen the production cels on Ms. Hillary's walls? She didn't receive them as Christmas gifts. She worked her way up using a lot of talents. Mr. Smith has friends on the board."

I wished I could say I was surprised, but humans are creatively resourceful.

"Noted. As long as you don't hurt the old man," I said.

Nurse Renee flashed a half-grin that disappeared as quickly as it had materialized. I was not sure how to interpret the smile. Was it an oddity in her "services" or what? Renee Blackwell was still on my "black" list.

The next resident we visited was semi-comatose, and Truman assessed the man's condition as non-interactive and turned back out the door. Truman preferred visiting people who were interactive. He led me to one of the small alcoves where residents gathered to socialize in small groups. Two elders chatted and played cards at a circular table.

"Truman!" One of the players reached out with both hands toward my dog, knocking the deck of cards on the floor. I played 52 Pick Up while the two residents petted Truman.

On my knees, I saw Mr. Smith come out of his room and join a resident I had never seen before. The man appeared to be Mr. Smith's age and alert.

I stacked the card deck on the table and chatted for a few minutes. Curious about Mr. Smith's new friend, I headed back that way.

My intentions changed as I got closer. Mr. Smith's animated conversation indicated I should not butt in. I smiled and walked by, giving them the opportunity to invite me to join their conversation.

Each man reached out a hand to touch Truman's back as we strolled by but did not show signs they wanted to interact with me. It lifted my spirits to see Mr. Smith engaged with a new friend. I worried about the effect Anna's death had had on him. They had known each other for years.

Since the men did not invite me to stop, I headed to Anna's old room occupied by the rich newbie. I stuck my head in the door of her room, it was transformed. Sunlight shining through lacy curtains sparkled on polished early American style furniture. An artistic reproduction quilt covered the full-sized canopy bed. An elderly lady wearing a lavender dress and a flowered silk scarf sat reading in a burgundy velvet chair.

"Hello, I'm Margie and this is my dog Truman. We visit residents here to cheer them up. Would you like a visit from Truman and me?"

Never lifting her gaze from her book, she said, "Please do not bring that dog into my room. I do not like dogs. They shed, and they stink."

I backed up. Truman mimicked me backing up too. I assumed, like me, he did not want to turn his back on this woman.

"I guess we can scratch that one off our list," I said to my dog.

I glanced up the administrative hallway and saw Juan entering Ms. Hillary's office. I wondered if she had mentioned to him that I was worried about him being involved with Meredith's death, and now, maybe Anna's death too.

We were half-way down the next hall and Truman headed toward the back door. He had to pee. I keyed myself out and hurried Truman to a tree on the far side of the lawn. He relieved himself, and we headed back to the building. As I reached for the keypad, the door opened. Juan walked out. An angry frown dominated his face, his shoulders were stiff, and his fists clenched.

"Hi, Juan. How are you doing?" I guessed his meeting with Ms. Hillary was not rewarding. I hoped Truman could cheer him up.

"Not good." He blocked the door glaring at me. He did not appear as if he intended to move.

"I'm sorry." Apprehension engaged my survival defense mechanisms. The shade on the door was closed meaning no one could see us. No windows faced the doorway. I was alone with this man. Truman was my only hope in case of a confrontation. Truman was standing behind me, his attention focused on a barking neighborhood dog. *Great protector, pup.*

"Why did you call me out to Ms. Hillary? What have I ever done to you?"

"I am sorry Juan. I shared something Anna said about Meredith. Then Anna died unexpectedly." *That's the good idiot confront a possible murderer, alone. Brilliant, totally brilliant.*

"Look lady. If you had accused me or murder a decade ago, to be cordial I would have broken both your legs. But I'm a new man. I don't hurt people anymore. I go to Ms. Hillary's church and she was kind enough to give me a break and this job. I would appreciate it if you did not make it hard on me by calling my character into question. I have been clean, law-abiding, working hard, and I have not given anyone cause to call me out for ten years. Now for no reason you do it. If you have a problem with me, talk to me first."

Juan claimed to be a changed person but his large muscular frame and his angry face intimidated me. I forced myself to breathe and reached down and stroked the top of Truman's head.

Truman glanced up at me, then focused on Juan. His eyes switched back and forth between Juan and me. Truman faced Juan and wagged his tail once, his way of asking for permission to approach someone. Truman did not seem concerned about Juan. Hoping to assuage the situation, I gave the hand signal to "go visit", and he walked right up to Juan who reached down and scratched Truman behind the ears.

What did I have to lose, besides my life? "I'm concerned with Meredith's death. Supposedly, she was getting better. Anna told me The Black One killed Meredith. Then maybe because Anna knew the killer, the killer killed Anna.

Juan looked slightly confused. "Go on."

"Truthfully, I did wonder about one thing. Since you are darker skinned, and wear dark scrubs, I thought Anna might be referring to you, and she was really was saying The Bl-"

Juan interrupted, "The Black Juan?" He laughed so hard he put a hand on the wall to steady himself. Truman wiggled and bounced. He wanted in on the joke.

I was a bit relieved but felt very stupid. "Sorry."

"Meredith and Anna were two of my favorites. I would never have done anything to harm them. They liked me and always asked for me by name. If someone did harm them, I would seriously consider returning to my old ways."

"Sorrier." My face turned red. I could not think of anything else to say.

Juan shook his head, keyed the door open and held it for Truman and me to go in. "Please, keep to your dog visits. They do a world of good for the residents and staff."

"I'll try." My gut told me Juan was telling the truth. My head informed me that if he was lying, then I might be the next victim. My heart reminded me that I was not a successful judge of character, and I needed to watch my back.

Down the corridor, the conversation between Mr. Smith and the new resident had slowed down. I approached them.

Mr. Smith leaned over and held both arms open wide, "Truman, old boy!"

Truman trotted up and wriggled in the old man's gentle embrace.

"Bart, meet Truman and his human, Margie the Mutt Manager."

"Nice to meet you." The old man reached his hand out to shake mine. I gently grasped it to sense his grip. I learned the hard way that because most elderly folks have arthritis, a firm handshake might cause pain. I allowed the older person to dictate the intensity of a handshake. Bart's handshake was softer than his smiling face prompted me to believe it would be.

Bart moved his walker to the side. Truman alerted on the tennis balls covering the walker's feet and shifted his weight and attention toward them.

"Come here, you silly dog," Bart said and clapped his legs, "Those are my balls, leave them be."

"You shouldn't be teasing that dog with your balls. That's unnatural," Mr. Smith joked.

A fleeting image crossed my mind. I shook my head to clear it.

"Bart's a former detective. I was telling him about what Anna said regarding Meredith's death. I still think Anna was on target about how Meredith died."

"So what do you think about Anna's death?" I asked to be polite. Juan's words where still fresh in my mind.

"Curious. I missed predicting that one completely. Makes me suspicious. But then maybe I'm getting rusty in my old age," Mr. Smith said.

Bart chimed in, "Bob here, was telling me about how Anna kept talking about the Black One being a murderer."

I had never heard Mr. Smith referred to as Bob, and it took a second to process. I nodded. "It could be coincidence."

"I may be old," Bart said, "but in three decades of investigating human wickedness, I learned to trust myself when I smell a rat. I'm not sure about this one yet. Could be coincidence, or maybe not. I'll do some follow-up. I'm going to pick this old fart's brain, which may be a messy business."

"You better believe it. This old fart will be glad to spill the beans."

The two men cackled so hard, I feared it would bring on a heart attack. Bart's arrival at Four Oaks was destiny. It was not my place to encourage or discourage this conversation, but I hoped they dug up facts that confirmed or dispelled my suspicions.

"Be careful. The folks here care about their image and they don't want slander or gossip. I would keep your investigation under cover," I said.

"We will take your advice. And anytime you want to do investigation under my covers just let me know." Mr. Smith grinned wide.

The two men fell into a fresh round of chaotic cackles. I shook my head, turned Truman toward the exit. It was time to go.

Before I could move off graciously, Lizzie Borden came clomping down the hall. "You two geezers need to get back to your rooms."

Her words shocked me, but her tone was unmistakably affectionate.

"Geezers?" Bart feigned shock.

The two men engaged in a diminished high-five, and then Mr. Smith asked, "What for?"

"There is some man here from the health department. He wants to interview people confidentially. He can't talk to you in private while you are sitting out in the hallway."

"Let this one take me to my room," Mr. Smith pointed toward me. He pointed to Lizzie then to Bart, "You can take the old fart, Bart."

The old men cackled. Lizzie cracked a rare smile. She nodded permission for me to accompany Mr. Smith.

In the room, Mr. Smith beckoned to me. "Come here a minute please."

I feared what he would ask me to do next, and for the first-time hoped Nurse "Lizzie Borden" Connelly would show up.

Mr. Smith pointed to a framed cel hanging on the wall. The main figure was Pluto. "If you like it, I want you to have that cel. It's not the most valuable one I have, but it's not the cheapest. I would be happy to have you put your name on the back. You said you like dogs."

"I couldn't. You are too generous," I said. In the back of my mind, I worried that he might ask for something in exchange, something I did not want to give.

"Okay, then. Put Truman's name on the back. I love that dog, and the image reminds me of him."

My heart melted.

"Truman's name, not mine?"

"If that gets me what I want."

I put my dog's name on a piece of blue tape and stuck it on the back of the cel.

"Thank you. See you next week," I said as I patted Mr. Smith's shoulder and left the room feeling a bit weepy eyed.

"I doubt it," Mr. Smith mumbled as I reached for the door. I turned saw him droop his head to his chest. I shivered.

Truman hauled me to the exit. When Truman said it was time to go, it was time to go. Outside, he relieved himself and headed to the car. Like their handlers, therapy dogs needed a break and rest. It was another one of those days. Not the best. They were happening more often than I liked.

Chapter 12

I needed alone time to decompress and process. Was there a murderer at the nursing home, or not? If so who? Why? The situation demanded comparing, sorting and discarding information. My head buzzed with bunches of small, disconnected thoughts. It was like opening a refrigerator full of leftover containers, none of them sizable enough to make a meal and no two of them complimentary. Somehow, I needed to discover how one thing could compliment another.

I plopped down in my fav-chair and flung my feet onto the hassock. The phone rang, and the caller ID named my son, Morgan.

"Hi, Mom. How's it going?"

I hesitated, drumming up a sociable flow of thought. I did not want to tell him about all the leftovers niggling my brain. "I'm okay. A bit tired."

"Take a nap." He was always practical.

"I might, but I'm not sleepy."

"Your Sjogrens getting to you?"

"Maybe, or maybe I've been doing too much."

"You're retired. Take a break and do something for yourself."

"That's what I was trying to figure out, what I should do." At least that much was truthful.

"Go for a ride, if you aren't too tired. I don't want you falling off and breaking something."

"The advantage of breaking something would be that I would have to give up on doing normal stuff and someone would have to come take care of me."

"Mom, are you trying to lay a guilt trip on me so I come visit you?"

"Absolutely not. I was thinking...never mind."

"Is there something going on that I should know about? What are you up to? Is there something, or someone in your life upsetting you, and you're not telling me about it?"

"No! Yes, there are a lot of folks and stuff in my life you don't know about."

"You know what I mean. Like a man who you aren't mentioning? I don't want you to get mixed up with someone who will hurt you."

Jerry did not seem the type who would intentionally hurt anyone or anything. I read him as a gentle spirit who was almost too boring and not risky enough to be interesting. My pause was too long.

"Mom?"

"What? I can handle myself." Our roles were reversed.

"Sounds like it is time for me to visit," Morgan said.

"I would like that, even if you are an overprotective son."

"You taught me well. For now, go for a ride. Pick a safe horse. You don't need a challenge today."

"I'll take Laurel out."

"Tell me about Laurel."

"Laurel is predictable. She's solid, easy to ride and happy to take me wherever I want to go. She is confident going out solo. "

"Sounds good. Hopefully she's not like that spooky thing you rode a few years ago. That one who refused to leave its friends at the barn and then threw you? Horses can be asses."

His doting was endearing.

"They're all equines and herd animals. A lot are nervous about going out with only a human and no other horses. It's a trust issue. If a horse trusts it rider, and feels like its rider is part of its team, then they're comfortable."

"So, don't you have to teach them who's boss?"

"Haven't I taught you anything? Horses feel safe when they are with trusted friends. Control freaks ruin frightened horses by using crops and spurs to scare them more."

"Scaring a horse seems counterproductive and dangerous. They might try to protect themselves."

"That's my boy. A horse dominated with fear looks for a way to rid itself of that fear."

"Laurel isn't quirky like Zanzu, that horse you made me ride, is she?"

"Zanzu was not quirky. You just grabbed him with your legs, so he ran. It's true, though, I have ridden some quirky horses."

"You are avoiding my question."

"The truth be told, like people, all horses have idiosyncrasies. They provide war stories to share around a campfire or while relaxing in the AC after a ride."

"You're avoiding my question," Morgan repeated.

"Laurel's quirk is she fears white objects."

"Like flowers?"

"Usually, bigger stuff like a white plastic grocery sack or a paper towel. Any freshly sawed log is suspect."

"So if you're on a trail ride and see a tree that's been cut, in an effort to get away, the horse might kill you?"

"If I'm driving down a narrow two-lane road, and the driver in the oncoming car is texting, it might kill me. Living life includes taking a little bit of risk. Fortunately, Laurel is the kind of horse who tries to help the rider get past the white specter rather than dump and run."

"That's comforting." Morgan inherited the sarcastic gene.

"I'll be fine. I will survive."

"Now you sound like my old mom."

"I'm not that old. Were all these questions about horses to distract me?"

"More like a mental health check up."

"You're a sneaky son."

"You taught me well." He chuckled.

We said our goodbyes and I texted Jeanine to make sure it was okay to borrow Laurel. I set off for the barn with Truman in tow.

The horses were hanging out heads drooped, a hind foot cocked in rest, and tails fluttering. I approached with a carrot in hand, and Laurel pricked her ears. Rochester's sagging eyelids conveyed, "sleeping, please do not disturb." I broke the carrot in two. I offered the small piece to Rochester who obliged me by opening one eye all the way and lipping the carrot out of my hand. I gave the larger piece to Laurel and slipped the halter on her head while she munched.

I brushed, combed, fly sprayed and picked Laurel's hooves clean, then wiped the dried crud on my hands onto my jeans. Grooming was the warm up phase of the ride. My muscles stretched and warmed with every motion. As a bonus, grooming renewed relational trust with Laurel. If I treated her with kindness and patience, on the ride she would reciprocate.

We headed to the wooded trail. Laurel knew it by heart. Barring an escaped ream of printer paper, we would have a relaxing ride. I only needed to sit the saddle, not really ride. I did not have to expend energy explaining to my horse where and how fast I wanted to go. Laurel knew the trail, where to go slow and where it was safe and fun to go faster. She knew how high to jump over each fallen log and what trip-hazard rocks to avoid. Truman was a pro at following or running alongside and not interfering with the horse.

Comfortably swaying in the saddle, and no humans within earshot, I talked to the horse about the first issue entering my mind. "I'm not sure if I want to get involved with anyone."

Laurel's ears flicked back to see if I was instructing her, or engaging in human babble. She determined it was the latter and her ears relaxed into walk-flop.

"Jerry's a nice guy, but I need to keep it slow. This relationship may not go anywhere, and that's okay. I have been okay. I will be okay."

Laurel snorted.

"What's that supposed to mean? Rochester is a gelding and that makes things less complicated for you, if you know what I mean."

Laurel shook her head back and forth as if she was saying, no. She was probably shaking a fly off her face, but I was almost suspicious she understood what I was saying.

For an hour, I rode on babbling to the horse and the trees. Truman's nose ramped his footspeed into hyper-drive. I enjoyed watching him off duty and playing like a dog. Laurel was taking care of me, so he had no worries.

On the return trail, I immersed myself in savoring the scenery. Strangling cobwebs cleared, negative possibilities desensitized, leftovers prioritized, I relaxed. I resigned myself to acceptable circumstances. Immediate threats extirpated, I was confident my friends were the resource that would help surmount any hardship.

Nature cleared my mind. Being surrounded by the timeless normalcy of the forest instilled a sense of calm. The tensions of human shenanigans were dislodged by the serene beauty of nature. This was a place where the struggles of life and death were eons old and accepted as the norm.

I loved trail rides. They grounded me and put my rampaging thoughts into perspective.

Chapter 13

Sign-in Sarah shoved a pen in my direction. I took it and signed the Four Oaks visitor log. We headed down the corridor. As we approached Ms. Hillary's office, the door jerked open startling Truman and me.

"Ms. Vonn." Ms. Hillary made a sweeping motion toward the interior of her office.

I bent over and whispered to Truman. "The queen requests our presence." I withheld a smirk and glided inside. Truman indulged my negative fantasy and pranced beside me, head held high.

Two men in dark blue polo shirts sat in the gray office chairs. Badge cases snapped to belts, and obscured picture IDs hanging from lanyards made it obvious they were there on business and not checking up on a relative. A representative from the health department had visited, maybe they wanted to interview me. I would give Four Oaks a good review.

Ms. Hillary marched to her desk and sat down. She clasped her hands and pressed them together until her knuckles turned white.

The men stood for introductions. The taller of them spoke. "Margie Vonn?"

I nodded.

The displeased frown on the other man's face did not go unnoticed.

"I'm Detective Lambert, and this is Detective Fournier. Have a seat."

Yes, sir, mister sir. Detectives? Had they found illegal activity here at Four Oaks? Meredith's death? Maybe.

"Have you had an acquaintance with Robert Smith?" Lambert asked.

"Yes." *Renee must have put her hand in the wrong place at the wrong time.*

"And Anna Longmire?"

"Yes?" I reached down to pet Truman and relieve my mounting tension.

"When is the last time you visited the Four Oaks Nursing and Rehabilitation facility?"

I was a bit confused. What difference did it make when I had visited? "It was about four days ago."

"What time did you leave the facility?"

"What's going on here? I can't remember exactly what time I left on any visits. How am I supposed to remember what time I left on that particular day? Do you think Truman or I swiped something? I sign the visitor check in and if I forgot to sign out, you can figure it was about an hour after that." Oops, my sarcasm control was eclipsed by my mouth.

Lambert spoke, his face a neutral mask. "We have you signing in four days ago, but you never signed out."

Whoopy Snoopy, so sue me. A memory popped out from a maze of thoughts. That was the day Truman had dragged me to the door so he could relieve himself. They brought in cops because I forgot to sign out?

"I guess I forgot to sign out."

"Can you tell us what time you left?" Lambert asked.

"I told you, I don't keep exact times. It was afternoon. I do remember leaving in a hurry. Truman had to go potty and the last thing any therapy dog handler wants is for her dog to relieve itself indoors. As you can imagine, it is a huge no-no to poop or pee on the floor. Why is this so important?"

"Of course, I understand, your dog had to relieve himself," Fournier said, but not like he believed me and not answering my question. He scribbled in his notebook.

Lambert leaned over and whispered something in Fournier's ear.

I could not keep my frustration bottled up any longer and my sarcasm gene climbed the ladder two notches.

"Look, I apologize for forgetting to sign out and taking care of my dog's needs instead of following protocol. I will promise that unless my mind is preoccupied by my dog's bathroom habits, I will be sure to always sign out. I would like to make my rounds now. I have plans for the afternoon." I stood. Truman jumped to his feet.

I considered my rudeness was enough to cause my dismissal as a volunteer, but this was so silly I did not care. Other facilities would be glad to have Truman and me visit. They would not be so upset by my forgetting to sign out.

"Sit down." Lambert pointed to the chair.

I glared at Lambert and remained standing.

"Please sit down, Ms. Vonn," Lambert repeated and stood up. "We are here on a serious complaint and would appreciate your cooperation."

I sank back onto the chair.

Lambert continued, "Is it true that on your last visit you claimed some of Mr. Robert Smith's memorabilia as an inheritance?"

I must have broken some Mickey Mouse nursing home policy. Or maybe Truman picked up a mini Minnie Mouse and ate it while I was preoccupied with writing his name on blue tape. I haven't combed through his poop since he was a puppy and swallowed my heirloom ring.

I took a deep breath counting in five, out five.

"Yes, I did. I did not think I was doing anything wrong. I will be glad to take my name off."

"What did you put your name on?"

"A little snow sleigh."

"Is that all?" Fournier asked.

I was a bit embarrassed. "I also put my dog's name on a cel, but Mr. Smith insisted that I do it."

"Uh huh, did he?" Lambert asked.

"Yes. So what is the problem? What did I do wrong? If I broke regulations, I apologize. I had no idea. I will be glad to take my name off of his stuff," I said.

Ms Hillary jumped to her feet, "You murdered him. For that stupid little sleigh."

My mouth dropped open.

Detective Fournier stood and walked toward Ms. Hillary, his arms folded across his chest. "It's okay. We'll handle it."

"What are you talking about? What is she talking about?" I asked.

"Mr. Smith passed around the same time you were here." The housekeeper who packed up Mr. Smith's belongings said that your name was on the sleigh. She said it had not been there earlier in the day when she dusted."

"Yes, I put my name on the sleigh during my visit that afternoon. He asked me to choose any one of his Disney things and insisted the cel go to Truman. The sleigh is a fast-food toy. It can't be worth enough to justify a murder."

"How much is enough to justify a murder?" Lambert asked.

I had chosen my words poorly. "Nothing! It was a cheap toy."

Ms. Hillary choked, "A cheap toy that most people assumed was covered with rhinestones. Mr. Smith must have told you about it. You spent a lot of time with him that day. You found out how much it was worth, you claimed it and murdered him. Or more likely, you murdered him, then put your name on it."

"What are you talking about? It's a fast-food toy someone decorated. It is only worth ten dollars at most. Unless you consider it folk art, then it could be worth twenty-five at the most. Besides, when I left Mr. Smith that day, he was alive."

Lambert turned to me. "Ms. Vonn, before you say anything else, let me explain that you can consider yourself under arrest. Let me explain how your rights are protected,"

He read the Miranda warning from a card.

"I am only going to say what is truthful, so I hardly need to protect myself from the truth. Mr. Smith was sitting in his wheelchair. His head was down when I left. I thought he fell asleep. Perhaps between the time I was talking to him and walked six feet to the door, he might have died."

Fournier asked, "So you are saying he may have died in your presence?"

"I didn't take his pulse before I left. I'm not a doctor, but I'm under the impression that if someone is talking to you, they are not dead. He appeared to have fallen asleep. I didn't try to wake him up."

Ms. Hillary turned her face down toward her desk, extending and clenching her fingers. Her head shot up. "That sleigh was not folk art. It was reworked by a jeweler. Those were diamonds, and other precious gems, along with gold. And it was a signed piece. The value is in the six-figure range. And that same day your dog," she pointed to Truman," inherited a very valuable cel. You couldn't wait to get your hands on the money. You had to push that gentle old man over the edge."

Exacerbated frowns crept onto the detectives' faces as Ms. Hillary babbled.

"You have probably been plotting this for months. When you finally got your name on pieces, you killed poor Mr. Smith. And Dr. Longmire died right after you left from your visit on that day, too! This is too much. You are ruining the reputation of this facility!" Ms. Hillary put her head on her desk and sobbed.

I was not sure if Ms. Hillary was crying because she would miss Mr. Smith or because she believed he was murdered, and murder would shower bad PR on Four Oaks.

"Why do you think he was murdered?" I asked.

Lambert wrinkled his brow. The slightly sweaty deep creases made his forehead look like molded wet clay. "We cannot divulge information from an open case. You will have to come with me."

My brain clicked into survival mode. I glanced at my dog. His wide eyes locked on my face, and his ears pulled back. He always knew when I was stressed. "If I'm under arrest, what will happen to my dog?"

Ms. Hillary lifted her mascara streaked face off her desk. "You can't leave that dog here."

"Can you contact someone to come get him?" Fournier asked.

"I can try." I reached down toward my doggie tote bag.

Lambert jumped to his feet. "Stop! One hand, and slowly, two fingers only."

"I need my cell phone if I'm going to contact someone. Unless you expect me to yell loud enough for my friend to hear me miles away."

I dug through my bag as Lambert watched closely. *This is absurd. Do you think I could pummel you to death with the bag of Barney Bear mini treats I have hidden in here?*

"Slowly, two fingers," he repeated.

I reached in and slowly drew out my phone with my thumb and index finger.

"See, it's a phone. I promise it's not a secret spy weapon that shoots lasers."

All three stared at me, faces blank.

I did not want to talk on the phone in front of the trio, so I texted Leslie. "Help! Please come get Truman at 4Oaks. Call me! NOW! Need HELP!"

We all sat in silence for two minutes. I stroked Truman. He sat up and put his head in my lap, his worried eyes reading my face.

Lambert slapped a hand on his knee. "You need to arrange for someone now. We can take the dog and secure him at the station if you can't get hold of anyone in the next five minutes.'

Desperate, I called Jerry's phone, but there was no answer.

"You have two minutes," Lambert said.

I racked my brain for whom else to call. I dialed the vet clinic. Someone had to be there. The receptionist answered.

"This is Margie Vonn. I need to talk to Jerry, right now."

"Dr. Elliston is with a client."

"Is Lynn available?"

"Let me see, hold please."

A moment later, Lynn answered the phone. "What's wrong, Margie?"

"I've been arrested for murder and I need someone to take Truman for me. I'm at Four Oaks nursing home."

"Arrested, for what?"

"Murder. And no, I didn't kill anyone. I need someone to come get my dog."

My phone dinged with a text from Leslie, "On my way. Calling you right now."

"Never mind. Leslie will take care of it." I hung up Lynn's call and picked up Leslie's. I explained my crisis and Leslie assured me she was in the car and rolling. I was thankful to have her as my friend.

The next 10 minutes were quiet as the detectives typed on their phones. Sour faced, Ms. Hillary stared at her computer moving and clicking the mouse. I sat stroking my dog who sensed my tension and yawned several times. I cried dry tears. Sjogrens Disease had destroyed my tear glands. Deprived of that natural response to overwhelming emotions, I cried internally with no tears to warm my face and help wash away the hurt. My gut burned.

Leslie arrived, hugged me, offered a word of encouragement and put Truman in the back of her car with Rusta. The detectives put me in the back of the police car and hauled me off to the city jail.

At least the cell was clean and neat, despite being old and cold. It was like an old-fashioned zoo cage with concrete block walls enclosing three sides. Three quarters of the front was barred in traditional incarceration style. A small wall to the side of the bars hid the toilet from the corridor. The cell accommodated two, but I did not complain that I was the only occupant.

For an hour, I sat on the bed contemplating 'why me' and what I could do to escape this mess. If I had done something wrong, I might have been able to backtrack and find a way out of it, but I had no mental map to follow. I had no idea what steps I should take to rescue myself. Except for TV, movies and books, I was not familiar with criminal court. Chalk it up to false confidence in due process, but although I was perplexed, I was not afraid of being found guilty.

I stretched out on the bed, covered myself, head included, and engaged my imagination. I pictured what it was like outdoors and took a walk in my mind. Exhausted, I fell asleep.

I dreamed of riding free and casually cantering across a cool grassy field dotted with colorful wildflowers. The distant sound of hooves pounding the ground caught my attention. A rider on a horse thundered toward me from behind. I could not figure out who it was, but I was afraid. My breaths came hard and shallow. I urged my horse into an extended gallop. I gasped as I heard the horse behind us getting closer.

My horse shook his head and the reins ripped out of my hands. What was wrong with me! I needed to hold on. My horse slowed back to a three-beat canter, and I heard the horse behind change to a canter too. I groped for the reins and out of the corner of my eye, saw the nose of the other horse pull up beside me. I turned my head. Jerry was in the saddle. His face was unreadable, his arms pumping the reins. He breathed hard from galloping his horse. He glanced toward me.

I leaned forward and squeezed my horse hard. His legs reached further, but he was too tired to pick up more speed. The other horse kept pace.

Trembling, I anticipated Jerry's face appearing contorted and cruel.

"Are you okay?" His breath rushed out and sucked back in. His face was hard with concern. "Can I help?" he asked.

My body relaxed. Fear discharged from the core of my being outward through my body and fell to the ground behind my galloping horse.

I shifted my weight back until the horse slowed to a walk. The horse was more than willing to comply.

"Yes," I said. "I didn't know who you were."

I startled awake at the heavy metal sound of gears tumbling in the door lock. The door squeaked open as I pulled the covers off my head. A chunky female guard pointed to the corridor, "You're out for now. Your lawyer will explain the details."

"My lawyer?" I did not have a lawyer, but I was not going to question freedom, so I stood up and walked out.

I signed out at the desk and walked into the lobby. Jerry stood next to a sepia-skinned man dressed in a gray suit and a blue tie. His short black curly hair and pencil mustache were frosted with white. I assumed the man must be my lawyer. He reeked expensive.

"I'm so glad to see you." Jerry grabbed and hugged me.

"If you had something to do with me getting out, thank you." My eyes moistened to the point of dripping a tear. For a Sjogrenite, a shed tear was gold, a rare reminder that our bodily functions were not completely extinguished.

"Margie, this is a friend of mine, Nick Turner. He's a criminal defense lawyer. He arranged for your release."

"Nice to meet a friend of Jerry's," Nick said. He reached out to shake hands.

I grabbed Nick's hand with both of mine, "Thank you so much! I don't know what you did, but it made a world of difference to my life. I'm not sure how I can pay you, but I will find a way."

"Don't worry about that." He glanced at Jerry.

My eyes followed his and Jerry smiled.

"He owes me. At least he says he does. We can talk about that later," Jerry said.

"Can we get out of here?" I asked. I feared the cops would change their minds.

"I'll drive you to Nick's office and he can explain things to you there," Jerry said. He laid a comforting hand on my shoulder.

"Thank you." Ecstatic, apprehensive and agonized all at the same time, I feared another unknown would materialize from out of nowhere. I was in a hurry to be in a safe place.

My freedom was a gift from Jerry. I had done nothing to procure it, and I had been helpless to help myself. Not your typical handsome hero or knight in shining armor, but Jerry had rescued me. I did not consciously make the choice, but I resented his successful rescue. Maybe it was overwhelming stress that launched me into defense mode, but I refused to trust that his intentions were altruistic.

Jerry held open his Jeep's passenger door. Another yellow flag, he was trying to impress me. I scooted in. I texted Leslie to let her know I was released, and that I would pick up Truman and explain what was going on as soon as I could. She responded that she and Rusta were happy to doggie-sit for us for as long as we needed.

Another rescue. A tiny wave of relaxation, rippled down from my head to my toes. I needed my friends.

Stopped at a red light, Jerry asked, "So do you think Ms. Hillary is in on it?"

"I don't know. The whole thing seems like a set up. I'm convinced there is foul play but I'm not sure what's going on. I can't figure out why they singled me out as a murderer, unless Ms. Hillary is trying to switch the blame to me. I know I didn't murder anyone, but I don't know if she did."

"Do you know of any reason Ms. Hillary would be jealous or how she could get money by killing Mr. Smith?"

My mind whipped around like an escaped fire hose and landed pointing to Ms. Hillary's office walls. "She has some valuable Disney production cels in her office. One of the nurses implied she got them from Mr. Smith for..." I hesitated, not sure how to explain what I saw without embarrassing myself or Jerry.

Jerry glanced at me, one eyebrow raised.

I soldiered on.

"It was strongly implied Ms. Hillary received them for favors rendered." I turned toward the window for an instant.

Jerry cocked his head and sent me an are-you-kidding smile. He chuckled. "Tell me more."

Downgraded to deer in the headlights, my mind blanked because of the blasted puppy-dog head cock.

Jerry's face was half-imp and half-empath. "It's okay. You don't have to. I'm teasing."

"Rat."

"Rats are quite intelligent animals."

I appreciated the casual teasing. It lightened my mood, softening my defensive wall.

"You said this lawyer owes you something. What did you mean?" I asked, considering potential financial burdens.

"Nick has a Portuguese Water Dog named Spotty. Spotty is usually obedient, but one day he decided to take off across the street. He didn't make it. A delivery truck hit him hard. He was my first client on my first day at my new clinic. I wasn't sure I could save Spotty, and I thought at best I would have to remove his leg. Nick asked me to try to save the dog and the leg. Long story short, Spotty is doing great with all four legs. Nick told me if I ever needed a criminal lawyer, he would be glad to help me. Of course neither of us dreamed that would ever happen, but," Jerry grinned, "here we are."

"What does that mean? Here we are. Thanks for the cut."

Jerry jerked his chin in and blinked his eyes.

"What I mean is we are here." He turned the Jeep into a parking lot in front of a new colonial style brick building.

An engraved sign, "Nicholas A. Turner, Attorney at Law," hung on the side of the gray cross-and-bible door. The building and landscaping reminded me of Colonial Williamsburg. I assumed the architect meant to give a first impression of patriotic justice. All I wanted was a decent lawyer who would not abscond with my life savings.

"Looks expensive," I said.

"I am sure he is. Don't worry about it."

"Don't patronize me."

Jerry shrugged his shoulders and gave me a side hug, holding on longer than a squeeze. "I'm trying to hold up a friend."

"Just so your lawyer friend doesn't hold me up."

"He won't. I promise," Jerry said.

Inside, leather chairs, polished wood, and authentic landscape paintings, shouted confidence and endurance. I braced myself anticipating this lawyer's subtle mind games.

We gathered at a walnut conference table. Handmade chocolate-brown ceramic mugs rested upside down on walnut coasters. A small matching plate accompanied each mug. Cornflower blue napkins folded like pockets, cradled wooden handled spreading knives. The decorative elements were poised to impress before a word was spoken.

A graceful young woman with a bright blue briefing bag slung over her shoulder brought in a food tray. A coffee carafe, a pitcher of cream, a bowl of sugar and one of honey filled the tray.

"Hi, I'm Crys." She placed the tray on the table and sat down. She moved the handmade cup off the coaster and pulled a tablet and coffee cup out of her briefing bag. The wording on the cup said, "Paralegal— Definition: A person who babysits lawyers."

At least these folks had a sense of humor.

A young man with intern written all over him, brought in a second tray with an insulated basket of warm bagels and a ceramic dish of mascarpone.

"The ones with the toothpick flags are gluten free," Crys said.

Nick walked in from a side door and gestured to the spread. "Don't wait on me. Help yourself, please."

Starving enough to grab the whole basket of bagels, I impressed myself and took the time to use the serving tongs to pluck one and place it gently on my plate. I heaped the bagel with mascarpone. My teeth slid through the creamy topping and sliced into the firm bagel. Heaven.

Nick nibbled on his bagel and sipped coffee while Crys presented the formal legalities of expectations. "Any questions?"

My mouth full of bagel, I shook my head, no.

"Margie, tell me about the last time you saw Mr. Smith," Nick said.

I washed the bagel down with coffee.

"When I left his room, he was in his wheelchair."

"And?" Nick prompted.

"He was sitting with his head down, like this." I dropped my chin to my chest.

"And?"

"Should I have called a nurse? Did he suffocate because his head was drooping, and I did not call anyone?" I asked.

Nick responded, "No, his neck was broken. They found him on the floor."

"Could he have fallen out and broken his neck?" I asked.

"Not likely. The autopsy is not finished. We will know more later."

Jerry's attention focused on me. His eyes softened, and his head cocked to the side. His smile and head nod were almost imperceptible.

Jerry was easy to read. Over the centuries, dogs evolved to have the ability to read subtle human body language. Jerry gave signals like a long time dog handler, his body communicating language with no words.

Nick referred to his tablet. "Tell me about Ms. Hillary. What is your relationship with her?"

"I've only talked to her a few times. Most of the time I deal with the activities director. I did go to Ms. Hillary's office to report that one of her residents told me her roommate was murdered."

Nick's eyebrows shot up and he jerked back an inch. "This is the first time I've heard about this. Please explain."

"Anna Longmire told me her roommate, Meredith Marshall had been murdered. Mr. Smith agreed with Anna that Meredith had been murdered."

"So were Longmire and Smith of sound mind?" Nick asked.

"I guess that is debatable."

Nick's introspective frown made me pause for a second.

"I'm not a doctor, I can't make a medical judgment call. They seemed to know what was going on around them," I said.

"That is why you talked to Ms. Hillary?"

I nodded. "I felt like I should tell her about Anna's concern. When I did, she didn't seem to appreciate the information. She told me to stick to dog handling."

"Do you think it would be worth it for me to talk to Anna Longmire?"

"She's dead," I said.

Nick's face went neutral. "So Anna said Meredith was murdered, and Mr. Smith agreed. You told Ms. Hillary and then Anna turned up dead. What about Mr. Smith?" Nick asked.

"Died right after that," I said.

"People do die in nursing homes," Jerry chimed in.

I threw him a heavy 'that is not helpful' frown.

"It's true," Jerry said.

"Yes," Nick said, "but these three people are linked by more than being old. They are in the same facility, and from what I understand, their deaths were somewhat unexpected. That could indicate foul play. Did you say the first person you think may have been murdered was Marshall?"

"Yes, Meredith Marshall."

"Why does her name sound familiar?" He addressed Crys as if she should know the answer.

She did. Pointing to the tablet Crys said, "I searched the web obits. Mrs. Meredith Marshall. Survived by son Ben Marshall, and granddaughter, Carley Marshall. Meredith was the owner of Colors of the Earth, the paint store where we bought all our paint when we remodeled this place."

"Ah, interesting. Very interesting." Nick pressed his lips together and they all but disappeared leaving it their place a tight fleshy line.

With no words exchanged, Nick nodded to Crys. She nodded back and tapped on her tablet.

"Do you know of any other relational links for the three deceased? Especially anything having to do with Ms. Hillary?" Nick asked.

"The three were friends. The most solid link to Ms. Hillary, is Mr. Smith."

I told them about the production cels, the sleigh and other memorabilia. I hinted at how Ms. Hillary may have obtained hers.

Jerry leaned forward, forearms on the table. "Since Mr. Smith gave you something very valuable, it sounds like Ms. Hillary could have jealousy and money motives. She may have felt like Smith's giving you gifts was stepping on her future. Especially if she wanted the items Smith gave you."

"Could have, are the operative words. I have no idea about their actual relationship. Ms. Hillary did go off on me big time about the snow globe sleigh."

"So are there any other possible connections that might cause issues?" Nick asked.

"There is some sort of odd connection between Meredith and her ex-son-in-law who was married to Carley's adoptive mother, something about a custody battle. And there is an ex-con working at the nursing home who is in tight with Ms. Hillary. Of course, there are a lot of other staff members. I don't have any idea how or if they could be involved." I explained what little I knew about the Meredith Marshall and Paul Wentworth connection, and told them about my encounter with Juan.

Two hours later, my brain emptied of all Four Oaks knowledge, we left. Jerry drove me to Leslie's to pick up Truman. The Jeep's loud road noise gave me an excuse not to talk. My throat was dry. A block away from Leslie's, Jerry broke the silence.

"Are you tired?"

That's the understatement of the year. "Yes."

More silence.

"Are you okay?"

Of course I'm not okay, you idiot. Keeping my mouth shut was a benefit of depleted energy.

"I don't feel like talking right now," I managed.

"Can we have dinner soon?"

I was irritable, but I owed him something. "Sure, give me a call in a day or two."

"Are you okay to drive home?"

I am okay enough to leap out of the car if you don't quit asking questions. "Yes," I said.

We pulled into Leslie's driveway. I scrambled out of the Jeep. "This will only take a second."

In less than a minute, Truman in the back seat, we headed to Four Oaks to retrieve my car.

"Thank you for the ride, and the help. Sorry I'm so tired and irritable."

"You had a hard day. Can I give you a hug?"

"Sure," I said.

I loaded Truman and headed home relieved I did not have to talk to another human being.

I got to the first stop sign and noticed my brakes were a bit spongy. I made a mental note to have them checked as soon as possible.

At the next four-way stop, I pressed on the brake, and it went to the floor. My HRV rolled through the intersection. A white SUV to my right had started moving forward. The driver laid a long loud blast on the horn. I hit the brakes again. Nothing.

My adrenaline spiked to maximum level. I steered toward a wide gravel shoulder on the far side of the intersection. I searched my memory on how to engage my emergency brake. Mississippi was so flat that in the two years I had my car, I had never used it. I spilled coffee on it once. It had to be on the console. I glanced down, saw the icon and flipped it up. I stopped on the gravel.

I cried my dry Sjogrens cry. Truman reached over the seat and stepping onto the console, snuffled my ear.

"I did not need one more thing today. Not one more!"

Truman licked my cheek.

"Thank you, bud. I'm so glad you are safe, but today I really don't care what happens to me."

I regrouped, tried my brakes and found them non-existent. I called Leslie.

"I need another favor. Can you pick up Truman and me at the corner of Westland and Shirley?"

"What's going on?" Leslie asked.

"Long story. My car broke down."

"You've had a hell-of-a-day. Hang on a bit. Leslie's taxi service is on the way."

I called the dealer and asked for a tow truck. Leslie arrived before the tow truck. I left the key on the visor. They had my phone number. I wanted to go home.

"You wanna talk about it?" Leslie asked.

"I don't have enough energy to talk," I said barely louder than a whisper.

We arrived at my house, and Leslie walked me to the door. Inside, she pointed to my fav-chair, handed me the TV remote, fed my critters and poured me a glass of wine.

"Call me if you need me again," she said and left without another word.

I thanked God for putting Leslie in my life. Our friendship was a privilege.

Chapter 14

Slouched in the chair at 2 am, I woke up to growls from my empty stomach. Truman danced in circles as I headed to the kitchen, approving of a mid-night treat. I handed Truman a piece of freeze-dried liver. The crinkling bag brought Caravaggio out of his hidey-hole. The look on his face was akin to, stupid human, it's about time you figured out the proper time to eat.

I hurt all over, a sign of an oncoming autoimmune flare. All the stress of the previous day turned my body against itself. My skin burned and itched. My dry mouth was stuck together, and my eyelids rubbed like sandpaper on my eyeballs.

I grabbed a cold piece of gluten-free pizza, wolfed it down with a glass of water and two OTC pain pills, and climbed into bed.

My cell phone woke me up at 10 am. It displayed Judith's caller ID. I still hurt.

"Hi, Judith." I headed to the kitchen for a glass of fresh water and my hydroxychloroquine, the malaria drug prescribed to ease my symptoms.

"Are you alright? I heard you were arrested for the deaths at Four Oaks. That must be devastating."

"It threw me into a flare. I have Sjogrens Disease, a sister disease to Lupus. It's an autoimmune disease. When I am stressed, I flare."

"I've never heard of it. My sister has rheumatoid arthritis," Judith said.

"All the same family."

"Do you need me to drive you to the doctor? I can help with that."

"No, I can probably ride this out. It's not my easiest flare, but it's not my worst. My body feels mangled but my brain is working okay."

"My sister get's brain fog. She's a bank president and it can knock her for a loop."

"I get brain fog too. Before I was diagnosed, my brain oozed from one foggy cloud to the next. Thought connections were ephemeral at best. It terrified me. I thought I was losing my mind along with my ability to connect, rationalize, and plan."

"That sounds awful. If you decide you need something, let me know. I called to ask about your arrest. What an absurdity!"

"Tell me about it. A total absurdity. I have never even seen a real life murderer! No chance of me being one."

"Do you think they were murdered? Everyone knows that folks go to nursing homes to die in comfort."

And I might murder the next person who says that to me. "Ironic, isn't it? My hobby is comforting people in nursing homes, and I end up accused of murdering the people who I was comforting. I guess because I work with dogs, maybe someone thinks I am a proponent of euthanasia. I may put down a dog who is in misery, but it is different with people. Besides, none of the folks who died were suffering."

I impressed myself by stringing two thoughts together.

"Are you sure you are alright? Can I do anything for you? Do you need anything else?"

I need help getting you to stop asking if I need help. "I need rest. Besides all this crazy stuff about my being accused of murder, I'm sad and angry that Mr. Smith was probably murdered. It makes me sick to my stomach. I appreciate your checking in on me."

"I'm glad to check in on you," Judith said.

"I do have a question," I said.

"What's that?"

"Did you get your dog from Paul Wentworth?"

There was a slight hesitation before she answered, "Yes, why?"

"Can I ask how well you know him?"

"Better than I wish I did. He's a jerk."

"Do you mind sharing with me? Remember Meredith, Anna's roommate who she said was murdered? Turns out, she was Paul's estranged ex-mother-in-law. I was wondering if you are aware of Paul's connection. I have a gut feeling that Meredith Marshall was the first domino in the murder of her, Anna and Mr. Smith."

"Now that you mention it, I do remember something about Meredith Marshall. I didn't realize that was the same Meredith from Four Oaks."

"And?" I prompted.

"Please don't judge me for this. I've since learned that Paul is a creep."

Another moment of silence passed. I waited.

Judith's voice cracked. "We were dating. I met Paul one day when he came in to do business at the bank where I work. He seemed friendly and kind. He was wearing a corgi t-shirt, and I told him that I had always wanted a corgi. He said he was a breeder and had a young adult he wanted to place. That's how we connected."

"You don't need to tell me all the gory details. I am interested in the Paul-Carley-Meredith connection."

"I was at his house one day and saw the newspaper's obituary about Meredith's death. The paper was folded open and on his kitchen table. I recognized the name from bank gossip. I mentioned to Paul that even though the Marshall woman did not have a lot of money, the granddaughter was going to be a very rich girl."

"Tell me more, please. This may be relevant."

"Paul said he knew the girl and asked me about her trust fund."

"Trust fund? How was he aware of a trust fund?"

"That's the thing. I don't know. I knew there was money from outside coming to the girl, but I don't know how Paul knew. Gossip maybe? A lot of so called private information flies in and out bank doors."

"Does your bank hold the trust money?"

"My bank has something to do with it. I'm not exactly sure what. I only heard rumors. Paul kept pressing me for information. The grapevine said it was a bundle, but I told Paul that it was only a rumor, and I didn't have any hard knowledge."

"What did he say?"

"He pressured me to try to find out solid information. He acted like it was only a casual interest, but I think he was trying to make me feel guilty for not sharing information. The pressure made me angry. I wasn't going to sacrifice my ethics or my job. I told him he could find out when the court settled everything. Our relationship deteriorated after that."

"Do you know if he ever visited Four Oaks? I thought I saw him there, but I can't be sure."

"Not that I remember. Wait. Now that you mention it, I do recall our having a casual conversation about it when I told him that I was going there with you. I think he may have visited Meredith there. I really can't remember. It didn't seem important."

"Thanks, Judith. You may have given me a lead. If you think of anything else, please, please, please call me."

"I wish I had more for you. I will definitely call if I think of anything else."

Angry and depressed, determined to avoid inciting my body's self-torture, I grabbed my laptop and plopped into my recliner. I clicked on my browser's "intellectual" folder bookmarks. I escaped to the world of academic articles. I needed to focus. As I matured, my addiction to Saturday morning cartoons was replaced by intellectual entertainment. The fact that my favorite cartoon show was the nerdy Mr. Peabody and Sherman, probably foreshadowed my current diversion.

For my article of the day, I searched "canine empathy" and read.

The next time I had dinner with Leslie, I would wow her with a new infusion of scientific facts about the deep connection between dogs and humans.

I spent the entire morning rotating from laptop, to TV, to deck. At noon, the dealer called about my car.

"Looks like somehow the hydraulic brake line came loose. Nothing's broke, it only came apart. We'll have it fixed by 3 o'clock."

I had no intention of leaving my house.

I settled in to finish reading the last two chapters of "The Genius of Dogs." Inspired to learn more about the extent of a dog's intelligence, I headed down the never-ending rabbit hole of dog training videos. I loved to see how others interacted with their critters. Online rabbit holes were my contemporary version of Alice, escaping from reality.

Leslie called.

"Hey friend, I'm on a grocery store run, do you need anything?"

Delivery service? I could exploit my disease if I was so inclined. "No, I'm taking it easy to day. I'm good but thanks for asking," I said.

"I your feeling up to it tomorrow, do you and Truman want to do Bullard Park? I'll run by and pick you up."

"I think tomorrow will be okay. It will give me a goal to focus on. Can we pick up my car on the way to Bullard?"

"Sure. See you at 10?"

"That works."

The rabbit hole spell was broken. I cleaned out a junk drawer. As a self-reward, I stretched out on the sofa to fractional binge-watch. I watched two or three of a series, then moved on to a different series. I floated downstream all day. Bedtime came early.

Chapter 15

The morning sun crept across my bed enticing Caravaggio to stretch out in a streak of sunlight. He wriggled into the brightest spot, and nudged my hand for pets. He was tempting me to write off another day. I would not cave. I had stuff to accomplish.

I scratched Caravaggio behind the ears, "Sorry bud, I'm feeling up to taking the dog out. I'll leave you to sunbathing solo."

OTC pain relievers, a cup of coffee and a hot shower removed ninety percent of the flare remnants. I was ready to move forward with the day. Monitoring my body a couple times an hour, if I recognized an oncoming reaction I could step back and regroup. Pushing too hard was counterproductive.

Leslie and I picked up my car and then took the dogs to Bullard Park. For my benefit, we sauntered rather than hiked. We took the short path through the woods, the exercise refreshing me. We emerged from the trees, and saw Tara and Susan with their families on the playground. Carley was with them.

"Truman!" Carley put her arms around my dog and buried her face in his neck.

"Margie!" Tara called as she waved. "We were just talking about you."

The younger kids took Carley's action as permission to surround the dogs. Rusta and Truman loved the multiple little hands rubbing their bodies. The happy massages provided the dogs with a bit of heaven on earth.

"I'm having a birthday party," Carley said. "I will be turning 13. I want you to come. You can bring Truman too, if you like. There will be lots of food."

"I would love to come. I'm not sure Truman would be a good fit. He may enjoy begging for food a little too much."

"That would be great. The party is super special for me. The lawyer said that my bio-mother left me some money and she wanted to throw me a huge thirteenth birthday party. I kind of wish that I could save the money for college, but I guess a big birthday party was important to my bio-mom. Ben and Tara are making all the arrangements. Tara said the party money wasn't enough to help that much with college, anyway. There may be a little left over to save, and I can earn scholarships."

"I'm sure you can. You are a smart girl, already planning the next steps in your life. I'd love to celebrate with you." I hope that even Paul Wentworth was not jerk enough to be after this girl's party money. It wasn't enough for college, so that knocked out money as a motive and more or less cleared Paul as a suspect.

"There is going to be music, dancing, and a lot of shrimp, and those little sausages in blankets. My favorites! Are you sure Truman can't come?"

"Toothpicks terrify me," I said without thinking. "I had a friend whose dog ate an hors d'oeuvre, toothpick and all. Before they knew it, the dog died. I try to keep Truman away from anything with toothpicks. He's a good one, but he's still a dog." *Well, nitwit, you certainly squashed the cheerful mood.* "Me, on the other hand, I know not to swallow toothpicks and would absolutely love to attend if it's okay for me to show up alone."

Tara nodded. "Sure. It's a gotcha celebration too. Because Paul abandoned Carley and her mom Olivia, Ben and I were awarded permanent legal custody of Carley.

"And we're excited to hear the lawyer read a letter written by Carley's bio-mom. She wanted it sealed until Carley's 13th birthday party. That's why she left money to foot the bill for a big party. Carley is so excited to hear the letter. The lawyer said it was full of hope and inspiration." She put her arm around Carley's shoulder.

"I'm so glad to hear you got custody." I wondered how Paul Wentworth took the news.

"I'm asking that instead of people giving me birthday gifts, they make donations to the humane society shelter. Everyone can give any amount they want, and no one has to know how much. There will be a giant doggie bank for cash. After the party, I'll give it to the shelter. If someone wants to make a big donation, they can donate directly to the humane society and leave me a note in the doggie bank."

"So is it casual dress?" I asked.

"It's at The Ensconce Lodge, which is a bit upscale, so a little more than casual." Carley pulled out her cell phone and scrolled through her photos. "This is what I'm wearing."

The dress was beautiful. Long sleeved, white and blues, the bodice was light blue lace, and the tea length skirt flounced with navy chiffon.

"It looks like it will be perfect for you," I said. I was a bit surprised at the formality of the occasion and wondered what I could wear.

"Push me!" The redheaded girl grabbed Carley's hand and dragged her toward the swing set.

Tara hesitated and dropped her eyes to the ground. Truman plastered himself against her leg, sensing she needed the confidence of friendly touch.

"I heard that there is some sort of issue surrounding Meredith's death," she said.

"You probably heard I got arrested."

"Yes. We want to make sure that you know how much we appreciate you and Truman checking in on Carley while she was at Safe Acres. And we wanted to tell you we don't think you had anything to do with Meredith's death."

"Do you have any idea why anyone would want to kill her? Or Anna? Or Mr. Smith?"

"I heard there were others who died unexpectedly. I assume it was a string of coincidences. It isn't unusual for people to die in nursing homes."

There it was again. *I am gonna die if I hear that one more time.* I nodded.

"Was Meredith getting worse?" I asked.

"No, that's the odd thing. Ben visited her that morning and she seemed much healthier. She was talking about going home."

"Sometimes folks have a burst of energy right before they die," Leslie added.

I shot her a thanks-but-not look. I sensed that Tara was avoiding my original question about who would want Meredith dead. I asked again. "But why would anyone want Meredith dead?"

"I'm not sure."

"Did she leave a large inheritance?"

"Ben will get his mother's retirement account. But we don't think Meredith would have inherited much additional money from Carley's birth mother. If there was, I don't imagine it would be enough to kill someone over, if that's what you're thinking. She left plenty for a big party. It seemed very important for there to be a big hoopla for Carley's thirteenth."

"And the bio-mom left some money besides the party funds?"

"We think so. The lawyer isn't allowed to divulge what's in the letter and will. But he did hint that we wouldn't have to worry about college. I haven't told Carley, I don't want her to be disappointed if it's not enough. College tuition has skyrocketed since her bio-mom died."

"I've never heard of a coming-of-age party like that, but it sounds like something that Carley will remember her whole life," Leslie said.

Tara nodded. "It is unusual, but I guess keeping the information in the letter and the will under wraps was probably to keep family feuds and rumors from surfacing. The whole situation is strange. The lawyer has no stake in the emotional side of it, but the firm would lose their fees if the terms became public before Carley's thirteenth birthday."

"It's all so mysterious. There must be deep reasons dictating the need to keep it concealed. Maybe a famous father?" Leslie said.

"I have no idea," Tara said.

"Does Paul Wentworth have a stake in any of this?" I asked to double check my conclusion about his innocence.

"I don't think so," Tara said. "But he has been making a nuisance of himself. He wanted to be named as Carley's official guardian."

"Why does he want to be her guardian now?

"Guilt, I guess," Tara said.

"Does Paul know about the letter? Could he have insider knowledge? Could Paul be Carley's real father?" I hoped my questions did not offend Tara.

"The first time anyone besides the lawyers knew about the letter was when Carley was five. It was after Carley's adoptive mother Olivia passed, and everything was legally turned over to Meredith. No one except the lawyers knew what was in the letter. Paul didn't have custody of Carley, so I can't imagine he knew about it."

"Did Paul ever have custody of Carley, at any time?"

"No. We don't know if he's mentioned in the will or the letter. Unless he has some secret source, he wouldn't know how much money went to whom. Like I said, Ben and I assume if money is involved it wouldn't be much. Meredith lived comfortably but not luxuriously."

I was not convinced. My mind throbbed with questions. If Meredith was the trustee of the bio-mom's money, how much money was there? If it was a substantial amount, how would Paul Wentworth know about it? What would he gain if he killed Meredith? The connection between Paul and the Marshalls was tenuous. Why did he want custody of Carley? Was there something more than guilt involved? The looming questions were still why would someone kill Meredith, and who the heck was The Black One?

One of Susan's toddlers tripped over a landscape timber and fell into the mulch. He screamed. Susan picked him up. His knee trickled a drop of blood. The boy screamed like his leg had been severed at the knee. Susan tried to console him.

"I need to give Susan a hand. He won't stop screaming until he gets the all healing lime-green boo-boo bandage. We do this every time. We'll see you at 5, Friday, at Ensconce." Tara trotted off to retrieve her first aid kit. The children followed like ducklings in a line, Carley bringing up the rear.

"Sounds like a fun party," Leslie said.

I groaned. "I don't have a decent dress. I have today and tomorrow to find something to wear."

"Do you want to check my closet first? Sometimes Don and I have to go to fancy parties for his job. I have a few outfits. They would be slightly used, but the price is right."

"Let's go." I said.

I easily found a perfect dress, and headed home.

The days ticked by and late Friday afternoon, I slid into the emerald green dress I borrowed from Leslie. I considered it a "cheater" dress. It shimmered with elegance but felt like a soft nightgown. It flowed enough that I did not have to worry about what it would reveal, or how it would hang when I sat or stood. I dusted off my black heels and ratcheted them on my feet. I hoped I could still walk in them. They would be a constant reminder that I was dressed up, not down. I donned two gold chain necklaces and droopy gold and pearl earrings. I was more dressed up than any time in recent memory. It looked like I was wearing a fancy costume, but I liked what I saw in the mirror.

I arrived at Ensconce, and a valet took my car. I hoped the young man didn't get too much gray dog hair on his black pants. I should have told him there was a sticky roller in the glove box. I headed up the lodge's rustic stone entry stairway, concentrating more on my feet than where I was going. I wobbled on one uneven step, and a hand from behind grabbed my elbow to steady me.

Jerry stepped up beside me and offered his arm. "My lady, my arm? You look great."

I wobbled again and clutched his forearm, feeling his muscle tighten as I steadied myself. He put his hand on mine and smiled. My head wobbled worse than my high-heeled feet. I mustered up a generic smile of gratitude. Then stupid took over.

"What are you doing here?" I asked.

"I'm Lynn's plus-one." He pulled his chin back, puffed out his chest, and cocked his head to the side.

"Lynn?"

"My sister, remember? She's a hobby cellist and is playing music here. The musicians were allowed to invite someone. She invited me. Is that okay?"

"I...of course."

"What are you doing here?" Jerry asked.

"Truman and I visited Carley when she was at the children's shelter. Truman was invited, too, but I didn't bring him."

"He couldn't fit into his tux?"

"Toothpicks. And I am having a hard time walking in these heels. One wrong tug on the leash and I would fall on my butt, so I left him at home."

"Wise decision."

We entered through Ensconce Lodge's huge oak double doors. The walls were rough-hewn boards, but polished antique furniture glimmered with beads of light reflected from the chandeliers. Extravagant flower bouquets erupted from crystal vases placed strategically on embroidered runners.

As Carley had said, there was food and lots of it. There were a lot of toothpicks, too.

Jerry exuded slightly anti-semi-formal-rebelliousness with his polished black cowboy boots and neat jeans. His concession to semi-formal was an unbuttoned charcoal-gray sport jacket. It revealed a black vest and light blue shirt open at the neck, no tie. Comfort emitted from every inch of him.

Did I look like an overdressed giant leprechaun? Before I bad-talked myself too much, I scanned the crowd and was glad to see a full spectrum of dress. I was mid-spectrum. Leslie's dress was perfect, so I stopped the self-criticism.

Lynn sat on a small stage playing classical music with two women on violins and a man playing a viola.

"They sound good, but it seems like a strange choice for a 13-year-old's birthday," I said.

"Give it a minute and you'll understand."

Two songs later, the transitions began. The music turned rock, then migrated to folk, then jumped to pop. The musicians did all with artistic expertise.

We grazed at the food tables as we listened to the quartet. The giant platters were uniquely labeled with fancy descriptions of specific characteristics of the food.

"Interesting labels," I said pointing to the platter in front of us. The sign said, Healthy Hors d 'Oeuvres. "That's somewhat of an oxymoron."

A tuxedoed man next to me turned his head slowly until he caught my eye. "Ben Marshall is a nutritionist. He is very conscientious when it comes to individual food tolerances and limitations. My company, 'Distinctive Delicacies,' is the only caterer in town able to meet his stringent requirements. When we say gluten free, we mean it. When we say vegan, we mean not a drop of animal. If it's sausage and cheese wraps, it's on a separate platter."

"We look forward to enjoying it," Jerry said, rescuing me from further embarrassment.

We loaded our plates from the hors d'oeuvre table and moved on to sample a few items from "Devil's Delights". I grabbed some "Gluten Free Fare" and Jerry added some "Mostly Meat". Our plates full, we ordered adult beverages and staked out our seats at a table near the back of the room. A few of Jerry's pet-owner clients stopped by to say hello. Neither of us were close friends with anyone else at the party. I was glad to have someone to hang out with.

"What's with the clock?" I asked, pointing to a countdown clock on a sidewall.

"Lynn said that there would be some sort of ballyhoo for the legal reveal. They were asked to prepare special music and play it at the exact moment the count went to zero."

"That's a little dramatic."

"Lynn thinks it was planned by the law firm to bring special attention to them. Whatever they have, it can't be public until Carley turns 13. The clock marks the second she was born."

"Oh, really? If the moment she was born was recorded, then the birth mother's name must be recorded, too. Hopefully by the end of the night, we can call her something other than bio-mom," I said.

"Good point."

A couple sat down at our table. They recognized Jerry as a vet and droned on about the valuable characteristics of their little dogs. Jerry was polite but he did not solicit any additional output from the couple. I grew tired of their expounding on the virtues of Peety and Posey, their two assuredly adorable Shih Tzus. Jerry's eyes glazed over.

Attempting to save us both from death-by-discourse, I planned an escape. "Jerry, there's not much time." I pointed to the clock with ten minutes left on the countdown. "Do you want to dance?"

The quartet was playing a lively pop song, indicating there would not be any touchy feely dance requirements.

Jerry's face appeared stunned for a minute, then he smiled, "Excuse me, please. I would like to accommodate this lovely lady's request."

"Lovely lady? That's pushing it," I said when we were out of earshot.

"I was serious about that."

I blushed.

"I'm a horrible dancer," Jerry whispered.

His breath moved my hair away from my ear. "Me too, but I was about to start throwing in 'little hairy dog' sarcasms, so I thought it best to remove myself. Besides, I thought you needed rescuing."

"Thanks, I did. I owe you one. But seriously, I have no idea what dance to do when."

"Watch what the other's do and follow that."

Jerry and I faked dance moves through a couple of upbeat pop songs, and they wore us down. The countdown clock showed 5 minutes 30 seconds and the quartet transitioned to a much slower song.

Jerry's expression pinched, his eyes were glassy. The music played on. We stood there staring at each other while the couples around us embraced in slow dance mode, and others sat down. The teens deserted the dance floor.

"I am sorry, did I say something wrong?"

"No," he said. His voice cracked.

Glued to the floor, I was not sure what to do when Jerry reached his hand out, took mine and pulled me toward him in classic slow dance style. I moved closer, but I was not sure how close I wanted to be, or how close he wanted me to be. Mentally, I was dancing a classic insecure approach-avoidance two-step. I could not read Jerry's face. He seemed to be in another world.

He glanced down at me. "Good song."

"Meaningful song?" I asked, surmising it was the music, not me that upturned his emotions.

"Yes." His eyes moistened and he shuttered, "Y-yes."

It felt right to put my head on his shoulder to offer comfort. I hoped he did not think I was making a move on him while he was vulnerable.

He put his cheek on my hair and whispered, his voice uneven, "'Aerosmith, I Don't Want to Miss a Thing.' I'll explain sometime later."

I nodded, relaxed, and we danced entwining the friendly warmth of our bodies as we moved slowly to the music. My mind wrapped around the seed of a notion that Jerry had something to offer to my life.

The song ended. The quartet revved up into standard celebratory music, allowing us to avoid the awkwardness of ending the intimacy of the slow dance.

Carley at his side, the lawyer stepped onto the platform where the quartet was playing.

"Good evening," boomed across the room accompanied by screeching feedback from the speakers. The lawyer adjusted his volume as the crowd gathered at the front of the shiny hardwood platform. The teens who sat out the slow dance weaseled their way to the front.

The lawyer tried again. "Good evening. Welcome to Carley Marshall's thirteenth birthday celebration. My name is Jason Hudd and I represent the law firm of Ashton, Hudd and Marcos. I realize you are all waiting for what I have to say."

Sarcastic brain engaged. *We are all always waiting with bated breath to hear what every lawyer has to say.*

"It is common public knowledge that Carley was adopted as a newborn. Our law firm has been holding information provided by her birth mother. Carley and the Marshalls are aware the birth mother has been deceased for over a decade. That is all I can personally reveal."

The crowd groaned disappointedly.

Are telling us you aren't going to tell us anything?

Hudd raised his hand to quiet everyone and continued, "Let me explain. Carley's birth mother wrote a letter that she wanted to be read publically at this celebration. It contains the content of her will. She also obligated funds to finance this party. I will now read the letter, dated 12 years ago today, on Carley's first birthday."

The crowd quieted. A few clapped. In the style of a queen's herald making an official announcement, Hudd opened the letter with a flourish. He read:

Dear Daughter:

First, forgive me for setting up this dramatic celebration. I wanted to make sure that Paul and Olivia had an exciting celebration for your 13th birthday.

Hudd stopped. "I will clarify. Most of you know that Olivia, Carley's adoptive mother, died five years ago. Subsequently Olivia's mother Meredith was appointed guardian. Olivia's ex-husband Paul Wentworth was estranged and retained no custody rights. You will see that the writer did not anticipate the tragedies affecting this family. She fully expected both Olivia and Paul to be involved throughout Carley's life. He read on.

My life's passion and livelihood has been writing dramatic stage scripts. I want you to know a little of who I was, and why you were adopted. I directed this gathering as I knew I could not be there in person. This is my last script, and I want to share the truth and reality of my choices and circumstances.

You must be wondering why I did not keep my own daughter. The story is complicated. Except for my own, I cannot tell you names. They will be forever hidden. I am not proud of what I am going to tell you, but it is a story of my love for you and embraces the drama inherent in life. This is my last show. Please know that this is my will. I will die very soon.

Your biological father was a very wealthy man. He was a widower and much older than me. We were not married. We had good times together, but we were not really in love. Admittedly, I've been a bit of an unruly free spirit.

Soft giggles rippled through the group of teens.

I whispered to Jerry, "I hope this stays PG-13."

He chuckled.

Since he was older and had already raised a family, he did not want to start a new family. He was very upset when I got pregnant with you. He wanted me to have an abortion, but I would not. When I told him I wanted to keep the baby, he broke off our relationship. He did not want to complicate things for his grown children.

My obstetrician discovered I had advanced breast cancer. I will not live much past your first birthday. Your father generously provided money to take care of "everything."

I arranged for a wonderful couple to adopt you at birth. I wanted you to live a normal life. To help out, I have some savings I will leave to you. It will accrue some interest over the years. I also invested $3,000 in stocks of a small company. It was a small gamble. I hope they did well. My lawyer said they would, but lawyers will tell you anything.

Hudd's voice trailed off when he read the last sentence. The crowd twittered. Hudd continued:

Until you are five years old, your adoptive parents will not even know that I have left you this trust. I wanted to make sure that their motives for adoption were purely for love of you. The reading of this letter is the first they will hear about the stocks, which knowing my luck, are insignificant anyway. I am sure your sweet, sweet adoptive mother and father will be good managers of your inheritance.

You will get my savings in three increments. The first increment was when you were five years old. Your parents would have received $10,000. The second will be at this celebration, your thirteenth birthday, and you will receive $20,000 to be overseen by your parents.

The teens gave Carley thumbs up. No doubt twenty grand sounded like a small fortune.

You will also receive the stocks in three increments when you are 13, 16 and 18. If the stock funds have grown, you can either invest or cash them in, which ever you and your parents decide is better.

Hudd paused. "I will explain the stocks after the conclusion of the letter." He continued reading.

The law firm of Ashton and Hudd,

Hudd stopped again, "We added Antonio Marcos as a partner four years ago."

"Who cares? Get on with it," I whispered.

Ashton and Hudd had orders to keep this letter and its contents sealed until your thirteenth birthday. Olivia has a good heart and I have no worries she will love you as if you were from her own womb. She brought you to see me many times during this horrid illness. At this writing, I am not well and I am not sure if I will ever see you again. I am very sick. I will leave you more letters if I can. If this is the last, you will know that I left you my heart and the best care I could.

When you are 16, I leave you $30,000 of my savings and one-third more of the stocks. You can buy a car and some nice clothes. When you are eighteen, you will receive $40,000 to pay for college and the remainder of the stocks. Use it wisely.

Your loving mother, always and forever watching down on you from heaven,

Magdalena Cortosa.

I whispered to Jerry, "That's a nice amount but not enough money to kill someone over."

"Not for most people."

Hudd continued. "Of course everyone knows that stocks go up and down. I can only tell you the value of the third that you receive today. The stocks are with Magic Moment Beverage Company."

A quiet rush of whispers traveled through the older crowd.

The lawyer's tone of voice changed. He fidgeted. He locked eyes with Carley. "Carley, my dear young lady. Twelve years ago, Ms. Cortosa only invested $3,000 in stocks. She did not want to chance investing all of her money. Today you will receive one third of the investment, the current value of one-third of the money originally invested. Ms. Cortosa purchased 60,000 shares of the Magic Moment Beverage Company stock at five cents a share. Today you get the value of 20,000 shares, one third of the original purchase."

Carley frowned.

A muffled voice emanated from the teen section. "We didn't know this was math class. She can do the math." The other teens giggled.

Carley rolled her eyes. "So at five cents a share, that means I will be getting a thousand dollars more, added to the $20,000 to make $21,000?"

The lawyer's head jerked back. His eyes widened. "No, dear. She purchased 60,000 stocks for $3,000. Today you do get 20,000 shares but at today's value. They are now worth $80 each."

Gasps spattered throughout the crowd.

Carley's forehead wrinkled and she shook her head as if she did not quite understand.

"That means that today you are inheriting about 1.6 million dollars."

Carley's face turned white.

The crowd clapped. Carley's friends grabbed each other and jumped up and down cheering.

"That's enough to kill someone over," I whispered.

Jerry nodded, "Sure is. Especially if the rest of the shares grow for three more years. At 16, Carley will still be a minor. The guardian will have access to a lot of cash."

Hudd waited until the crowd quieted. "There is no guarantee of the value of the remaining stocks when you are 16 and 18. I advise you to seek guidance and invest these funds wisely."

"Typical lawyerly advice, especially if the firm gets a cut." My sarcasm had a voice. Poor Jerry.

"I'm sure they do get a cut. Ben and Tara look a bit stunned."

"I bet they are."

Tara and Ben stood at the far side of the group of family and friends surrounding Carley. Folks vied for Carley's attention. The teens were maintaining their cool and hanging out as close to Carley as they could get.

"Let's make our way to the door. Unless you want to stay to congratulate Carley," Jerry said.

"We can talk to her later. She's overrun with well-wishers."

Jerry took my arm.

"We can catch Tara and Ben later, too, when it's not so chaotic," I said.

On the way to the door, it dawned on me that Jerry and I had not arrived together. Goodbye-awkwardness loomed larger with every step down the stairs. I mulled over something significant I could say to end the evening. It was for naught.

"I have to admit, I find myself being a little jealous of the girl," I said.

"I know what you mean. I'm happy for her. A windfall like that will reduce a bunch of the stresses of modern survival. She won the lottery without even buying a ticket."

"True! It's wonderful. But already at her young age, she has paid her dues. She had a rough go of it and still maintained care and compassion for those around her. She's a great kid."

"And we did get to have fun at the party."

"It was eventful. I've got to hand it to Magdalena, her last script was powerful," I said.

"Agreed. The party was spot on. Seeing you here made it perfect," Jerry said.

A shield of caution materialized from my insecurities, reminding me of my past failures in judging human character. I hoped that I could proceed with caution and at the same time contribute to the forward motion of this relationship.

"I enjoyed sharing the evening with you." I surprised myself with my boldness and lack of sarcasm. I put one foot out of my comfort zone.

Chapter 16

In the dog show world, today's Paws in the Park affair was considered an unsanctioned fun event, as opposed to an official show event. The fun event allowed people to socialize and practice dog show activities. Charlotte organized Paws in the Park as a precursor for the huge June event, Hound Dog Pawty in the Park. The Pawty would host serious, sanctioned competition dog show events. Paws in the Park was much less stressful for everyone. Unlike official competitions, there was no entry fee. Donations to the shelter were appreciated. All dog owners were welcome, even those with puppies—vaccinations required. The event catered to all types of dog owners, from competitors to owners who only wanted to play with their dogs.

Charlotte had billed the event as BYOT&T—Bring Your Own Treats and Toys. A variety of activities were available for people and their dogs to experiment with and discover one that was fun for both. It was billed as a howling good hoopla. The sun shone, and a soft breeze created almost-cool temperatures. It was perfect for dog play.

Charlotte had arranged for a few supervised stations set up with specialized equipment. These stations included items for temperament testing, agility, obedience, and flyball. The dock on the lake had passed a safety check and was opened for dock dog retrieving. On land, eight bales of hay were stacked with tunnels to form a mini, barn rodent hunt. A large grassy area offered practice for dog sports that needed space but used little equipment. Trick dogs, conformation dogs, disk dogs, and retrievers played in that field. A Boy Scout troop ran a canine orienteering short course through the woods.

Leslie and I led Rusta and Truman to the agility equipment. A boxer and a small mutt were jumping and trying out the see-saw. Since it was informal, we rotated around the obstacles without getting in each other's ways. Truman and Rusta lost focus and wanted to play with each other, so we walked toward the lake and took a break on a park bench.

"Charlotte may be an irritating busy body, but she sure knows how to throw a dog party," Leslie said.

"She's a regular Dr. Seuss, 'It's a dog party. A big dog party,' I can't wait to see what the Hound Dog Pawty in the Park, will be like," I said.

"Look, there!" Leslie pointed toward a chocolate Labrador dragging its bearded owner toward the lake. "There's Rusta's brother. I've got to go say hello. Rusta and Peter Pan would love to play with each other. You want to come?"

"Thanks, but no. I need to rest and pace myself. You go. We can meet up later."

Leslie trotted off. Rusta leaped in circles almost dragging Leslie off her feet.

Truman turned to me, his eyes hopeful. "Sorry boy, you're stuck with a disabled lady. At least you aren't staked out on a chain in someone's backyard. Come on. Let's go do some easy tricks."

At the word "tricks" Truman stood up, ears pricked and head cocked. We headed along the parking lot and I spotted Paul shoving one of his corgis into a crate in the back of his van. I was still angry about him not paying Jerry. I could not help myself. I had to say something.

Paul's back was toward me. The rear of the van was open, and he was organizing collars and leashes. He draped two green leashes over his arm.

"Excuse me." I tried to make my voice authoritative, but the breezy day, and a lot of talking had dried my throat and salivary glands past their functional point. The words squeaked out like a coughing blue jay. I turned red.

Paul turned around. He was almost too cute to scold, but I pressed on. I did not like this person, no matter how much he resembled Tom Cruise. I took a sip of water and harnessed my voice.

"You said you were going to pay for Truman's vet bill, for the damage your corgi did."

"Your dog looks fine to me." He pushed his shoulders back and twirled one of the leashes.

"He is. He recovered fast, thanks to Jerry's doctoring."

"So you still think I need to pay?"

"You said you would."

"How much was the bill?"

"Including everything, a hundred." I had no idea how much the treatment cost, Jerry would not take my money. I figured a hundred would cover it.

"That's absurd. I'll pay half of that. You're gullible, and that man is taking advantage of you."

"You're overrated," I snapped.

Paul smirked squinting one eye. "You don't know me at all."

"I know more about you than you can imagine." The attack dog voice in my head urged me on. The comfort dog voice on the other side of my brain warned me to calm down. I chose attack dog.

"You are scum. The only reason you wanted Carley to live with you was so you could have her money. I wouldn't be surprised if you were involved in Meredith's murder." My mouth was as out of control as an unmuzzled Jack Russell in a hurdle race.

His mouth twitched enough to make me confident I had hit close to the truth.

"Meredith died from pneumonia. She was old."

"And then her friend Anna died unexpectedly, and then their mutual friend Mr. Smith died. I suppose you think those were coincidences?"

"I don't know what you are talking about. That's what old people do in nursing homes. They die. I don't think any of them recover from old age and go home to live another 50 years." Paul turned back toward his van.

"Look here, mister. You listen to me."

Paul dug under the pile of towels and pulled out something small, his body blocked my view of whatever it was.

"You are a deranged idiot," he said, his back still toward me. He gestured with the leashes dangling from his arm making a circle motion near his temple.

I grabbed one of the leashes and tugged to get his attention.

He spun around, seized my arm and twisted it. "Don't touch me!"

A rough tangled sound produced by Sjogrens-dry-throat escaped from my throat. It started as a mouse squeak then undulated to a cow groan. Before I recovered enough to tell him to let go, a flash of floppy eared gray, black leaped up and latched onto Paul's arm. Paul let go of me and took a swing at Truman who veered to the side fast enough to avoid the fist.

I jumped back, pulling Truman out of reach.

The item Paul had dug out from the towels was visible in his hand. It was a money clip filled with folded one-hundred dollar bills.

"Your therapy dog is going to lose his credentials for attacking me. I will see to that," Paul muttered.

"I don't think so. He was protecting me from violence".

"I was protecting myself from you, when you tried to hit me. You were trying to get in my van to steal my money."

"You liar! No one will believe your lies." I was dizzy from anger. I feared I would pass out. I entered that black space that occurs when trauma slams a person into freeze-brain.

A familiar voice rose up from behind me and brought me back. "I believe anything Paul says, and I saw your dog bite him."

I whipped around. The sight of Crazy Ingrid discharged a massive shot of adrenalin and reengaged my brain.

"Then you need glasses. My dog was protecting me." I scrutinized Paul's arm. The sleeve was not torn, so I knew his skin wasn't broken. Truman was helping to protect me, not trying to injure him.

Ingrid sneered, "What I saw was you trying to steal Paul's money clip. He was trying to keep you from taking it and your dog jumped up and bit him, unprovoked."

Paul smiled. "That's exactly what happened. I was trying to give her money to pay for a vet bill and she tried to take my whole clip."

"How can you live with yourselves? You are both idiot liars."

"That's better than being incredibly rude and a petty thief, to boot. First my wheelchair, now Paul's money. You have bad character. I would have thought better of you." Ingrid stuck her chin in the air.

"Get the hell out of here and stay out of my life," Paul said.

"Done!" I do not know if it was instinctive survival mode, or my inability to grasp the absurdity of the situation, but I turned and walked off.

His tail between his legs, Truman kept looking back over his shoulder. I had no remorse that I had just lied to Paul and Ingrid. I was not done with Paul but I was determined not to let him ruin my time at this event.

Rampant adrenaline launched me with a boost of energy. Truman and I attacked the remaining stations one at a time until I wore down. Finally, I relaxed and we had fun.

Leslie caught up with us as I was testing Truman's predisposition to flyball. He had none.

"Having a good day?" Leslie asked.

"Don't ask."

"Okay, where are you headed next?"

"The dock's open."

"Let's go. I'm sure Truman would like a swim." I wanted to tell her about my encounter with Paul and Ingrid, but it needed to be in a quiet place with no one around.

At the dock, a couple joined us. Their hyper Lab mix whined incessantly begging to get into the water. The man threw a ball and the dog flew 20 feet off the dock.

"Nice. Have you been working with him long?"

"First time." The man beamed as the dog returned the ball to his partner and dowsed her with lake water.

"He has potential," I said.

Truman and Rusta enjoyed several non-impressive launches from the dock. The Lab mix increased his leap distance with each try.

Leslie and I leashed our dogs and encouraged the couple to talk to Jonnie the dock dog trainer. We wandered around checking out other stations, but I did not have the courage to bring up the Paul-Ingrid thing.

We approached the vet station where three very focused women were watching Jerry demonstrate how to wrap an injured paw. An unfamiliar feeling irritated me, I tried to locate its source so I could reason it out of my head. Was it jealousy? We watched for a moment, waved and left.

I was spent. Too many emotions were surfacing unexpectedly. Weather seemed like the only reasonable conversation I could carry on with Leslie without jettisoning too much emotional ballast and causing my head to explode.

"Something is bothering you, friend. You're trying to have a good time, but something's distracting you. Do you want to talk?" Leslie asked.

"The event is wrapping up, I'm tired. I need a nap."

"Don gets home late tonight. After you take a nap, do you want to meet me for dinner? We can talk."

"Sure." I was too exhausted to think, but I would do whatever it took to move forward.

Chapter 17

I pulled up to my house and saw Rocky in the barnyard playing with the baby goats. Sitting on a hay bale with his head bent over his knees, Tyrion and Thumbalina teetered on his back. R2-D2 stood on the bale next to him and Tangina stood on her hind legs trying to butt R2-D2's head.

I walked over to collect some baby goat kisses. Truman followed, sniffed the goats, then engaged Tangina in a romp.

"I saw Leslie drop you off the other night. Are you having car problems?" Rocky asked.

"Brakes," I said, not wanting to revisit that stressful event.

"Brakes? That car is too new for brake issues."

"Something about the brake line coming loose."

Rocky sat up, his face in a thoughtful frown. "What? You know I tinker with cars a lot, but I've never heard of a new car's brake line coming loose. That sounds like a lawsuit in the making, maybe even a class action suit. Did you do a web search to see if yours was an isolated incident or if it has happened to other people?"

"No. I didn't think about it."

"Lines don't come loose by themselves."

"I'm afraid mine did." I scratched R2-D2 behind his ear. He leaned his head into my hand.

"I hope you didn't make someone mad enough to try to kill you. Brake failure is a common method to off someone."

Rocky was joking, but I paled. I was glad his eyes were fixed on Tangina who had stopped in front of him and threatened to butt him in the groin. I had not told Jeanine and Rocky about my Four Oaks debacle and jail experiences. I did not want my landlords to question my character or sanity.

"Not that I know of," I said.

I played with the goats for a few more minutes then headed to my house to nap.

After a good sleep, I showered, pulled on some clean jeans, donned a sociably acceptable casual shirt, and set off to meet Leslie at Horatio's Home Cooked.

We ordered an appetizer and sipped wine while we waited for dinner to be served.

"You didn't say if we were doing connect the dots tonight," I said.

"Let's talk about other things tonight. I'm guessing you could use a break from talking about death and such. I didn't bring our dot picture."

"We can always keep track of the numbers and draw them in later."

"Do you want to talk about it?" Leslie's tone indicated that she did not.

"Not really. Let's skip it tonight."

"Good, because I want to hear all about Carley's party. Did you talk to anyone interesting?"

"Maybe."

"Cough it up girl. Give me the juicy details." Leslie put her elbows on the table, and rested her chin on her clasped hands.

"Jerry was there."

"Did you sit with him?"

"Yes." I had a memory flash of his warm body against mine while we danced. I hesitated to share my fluctuating feelings about that. I was in right-brained goulash.

"You're holding back, friend. I'm asking you point blank. What happened?"

"Carley inherited a bundle."

"Duh. Everyone in the state knows that by now. You are trying to put me off. Did he go home with you?" She winked.

"No!"

I was relieved to see Charlotte walking toward our table. She waved as if she was patting the top of an invisible Great Dane's head. She carried a huge tote bag slung over one shoulder. When she got closer, a little shiny black nose sniffed the restaurant air through the side scrim panel.

Our dinner arrived the moment Charlotte sat down with us. The waitress paused next to Charlotte.

"Bring me a glass of pink Zin," Charlotte said.

The waitress rolled her eyes and left.

"How are you girls? I'm meeting a friend here, but I'm a little early," She patted the Inky bag. "So, I thought I would have a glass of wine while Inky and I waited. This is perfect. I'm so glad to see you."

"I'm glad to see you, too, Charlotte," I said. I saw Leslie almost choke on a sip of merlot. "There is something I wanted to ask you about."

"What is that, sweetie?"

"I think you know a man named Paul Wentworth."

"Yes."

That was one of the few times I heard Charlotte give a one-word answer to any question. For comic stress relief, without permission my brain imagined her in a doctor's office. *Does that hurt? Oh, yes it hurts at 3am but not as bad as 2am, and maybe about the same as after lunch.*

I refocused. "What can you tell me about him?"

"Why?"

Call Guinness Book of World Records. Two, one word responses in a row. "I had a disagreement with him at Paws in the Park. He seems hard to get along with."

That sparked Charlotte's fire. She launched into chatterbox mode.

"Oh, sweetie, if you are considering him as a paramour, take my advice and don't. I was afraid for Judith when she started getting involved with him. I think that dear woman saw the light, or should I say dark, very quickly."

Charlotte took a sip of wine. Leslie and I sat back mentally sifting through the information.

"I hate to have to admit it publicly, but he's my second cousin."

"I take it that you are not fond of him?" I asked.

"Sometimes I wonder about the way he treats his dogs. He always had a dark side. He was perfectly delightful when we were little, then all of a sudden BAM, he was horrible."

"Male puberty idiocies?" Leslie asked.

"Maybe. When we were kids, we had mean nicknames for each other. He called me Miss Piggy. He was horribly mean, so I called him The Black One."

I choked on a sip of wine. Leslie thumped my back. Charlotte continued without a pause.

"It's not PC now, but I wasn't referring to his color. I was referring to his dark, evil soul. He used to pull the heads out from the bodies of grasshoppers and let the heads dangle by the cord or veins or something. He would stick them right into my face. It was so gross."

"Stop!" I said. Her deluge threw my info sifter into disarray.

"Sorry, not meal time conversation, is it? I apologize. Let's talk about the Bahamas. I'm planning a trip--"

"Stop!" I raised my hand like a traffic cop.

Charlotte's eyes widened.

"I need to ask you something."

"Oh?"

That makes three. Truly a record night.

"Does anyone else know you called Paul, The Black One?" I asked.

Charlotte stared at us for a few seconds. "Why of course. All the kids called him that. They thought it was funny. Except for maybe cousin Br--"

I raised my hand stopping the traffic flow from her mouth.

"Did any adults know?" I asked.

"I don't think so."

She had slowed down to four words. *Not for the record book, but definitely an honorable mention.* I hoped I had chanced upon a method to steer the conversation. I envisioned a handheld stop sign for future conversations.

"Are you sure?" I asked.

"Why are you asking me about this?"

"Charlotte, this is important. I can't tell you why, but I need you to think back and try to remember if anyone except the kids knew Paul was called The Black One."

Charlotte leaned back, her eyes intent, flickering back and forth between me and Leslie. Leslie and I remained quiet. It was obvious she was searching her memory banks. Leslie and I sipped wine.

Charlotte fiddled with her glass. "The only time I ever remember mentioning that name to an adult was in high school. It was about hope. People can be so cruel to each other, and sometimes they only do bad stuff so they can feel like they have power. I wrote about how I had hope in spite of evil people around me."

Leslie and I exchanged eye rolls. It seemed my head would implode in an effort to extract significant bits of information from Charlotte's sea of jibber-jabber.

Charlotte sat quiet for a minute. I slowed my breathing.

"The title of my story was *The Black One*. The teacher called me up to her desk after class. She said it was a hard subject to read about, but that it was a very good story. It was the only A I ever got in literature class."

"We appreciate your sharing that with us," Leslie said.

Charlotte let out a huge sigh. "The teacher asked me if the evil character was based on my cousin Paul. He was in one of her other classes. I told her he had inspired me. She assured me it would be our secret to the end."

"It must have been a good story for her to recognize Paul as the real character. You must be proud of that A. They are hard to earn," I said.

"Yes," Charlotte sighed again. "I was honored by the A. It meant a lot to me, especially because my teacher became something of a literature expert. She ended up getting her PhD and teaching literature at Lorettina College for Women.

"Wait." I put my hand on hers. "Was that teacher Anna Longmire?"

"She was Anna Murphy when she taught at the high school, but she did marry someone named Longmire."

Leslie tilted her wine glass and poured the last gulp down her throat.

"Thank you." I patted Charlotte's hand.

"You have got to tell me what is going on." Charlotte put her hands on the table and bobbed her body up and down. "Please!"

"I'm so sorry. You have given us a very important piece of information. Don't share this with anyone, except the police if they ask you. Your life may depend on it."

Charlotte shrunk her shoulders down. "Paul?"

"I won't say anything else. Please, please do not talk about this at all," I said.

"Okay. Oh, look, my friend is here. Nice chatting with you." Charlotte took her Zinfandel and her covert canine carrier across the restaurant and sat at the table with her friend.

"I hope she can keep this quiet," Leslie said.

"Me too. A most interesting conversation. I would say that Paul is our man."

"But we have no real proof. 'The Black One' is not the most unique nickname. It could apply to a lot of people."

"You said you didn't want to talk about the murders, but we need to talk to Judith. She dated Paul, so she may have another piece of helpful information."

"You don't like Paul do you? There is no 'innocent until proved guilty' in your mind."

"Not since he tried to punch my dog."

Chapter 18

The next morning, I waited until a reasonable time to phone Judith. The phone rang three times and Judith answered.

"Hi, this is Margie. I have a couple of questions about Paul Wentworth. Would you mind talking with me about him?"

"That bacterium? I would rather not. If you are considering getting involved with him, I have one word, RUN! Don't get near him."

"Sounds like bad memories. I think he might be a key to a couple of deaths at Four Oaks. Do you remember talking to Anna, the lady who kept saying that her roommate Meredith had been killed? Anna ended up dying suspiciously. I'm trying to find out if there is some sort of connection with Paul."

There was silence except for clicking fingernails.

"Judith?"

"I'm thinking."

I waited.

"I made some mistakes and I might lose my job if I confide in you," Judith said.

"Oh. I see."

"I guess telling you that much means I have already made a decision to talk. I'm thinking out loud. If you tell the cops, they may haul me in. If that happens, I will have to tell the truth, anyway."

"True," I said.

"What if what I did unintentionally caused the deaths at Four Oaks?"

"Judith, if you did nothing intentional and you are connected in any way, it's because you were duped."

"I'm glad being stupid isn't illegal."

"We've all been tricked by someone. I hope no one would press charges against you. You're innocent of wrongdoing. Please, talk to me."

"I hate to be connected."

"I won't mention your name. I can ask the cops a hypothetical question about whether or not you could receive amnesty."

"That would be good, but it won't help me keep my job."

"True. But like you said, it's too late now. I don't think you want to stay silent and contribute to having a murderer running free. If in fact Paul is the killer."

More silence.

"I should have listened to my gut. I had a fuzzy feeling in my gut when I met him. Bad fuzzy, not good," Judith said.

"I'm not the world's best judge of character myself. I would run off with Jack-the-Ripper if he smiled nicely at me."

Before you trust someone and spill your guts, spend time with them first. Be cautious. If you have an inkling of doubt, move slowly. Do not imagine that you understand a person before you have spent a lot of time with them. I repeated my mantra in my mind.

The possibility of Judith pretending she did not like Paul crossed my mind. She could be trying to obtain information from me. I could be Paul's next victim. Judith could be in on the whole thing. I was proud of myself for applying the brakes and not divulging all the facts.

Judith sniffled. "I told you that I met Paul at the bank. He recently moved back in this area from Memphis, and he wanted to open a bank account. He saw my desk picture of my old Corgi, Dexter, who trotted over the Rainbow Bridge a year ago. We talked Corgi and one thing led to another and we ended up going out a few times."

"That's innocent enough."

"He asked me a lot about banking stuff. Of course, I thought we were making small talk. I never mentioned anyone's name. I remember telling him a lawyer had visited the bank. I told him I overheard the lawyer talking about a local girl's inheritance and how happy she would be on her 13th birthday. Paul asked me exactly how happy she would be, and I told him she would be set for life."

"But you didn't mention any names?"

"No."

"Did he ever talk about Meredith?"

"I did see her obituary on his table, but we really didn't talk about Meredith. Not that I remember. Do you think he knew her?"

I caught myself before I threw out too much information. Maybe she was innocent, but she might be fishing. Was I being paranoid?

"I'm not sure what he knew about Meredith," I said. "If you think of some solid connection or anything else that might be helpful, phone me."

"What are you going to do with the information I told you?" she asked.

"I'll mull it around in my mind for a bit and try to see if I can come up with something solid. But thank you. Can I call you if I have more questions?"

"Sure, or we can meet somewhere and talk."

Like some dark alley? I realized after I hung up, telling her I was going to take time to think was the dumbest thing I could have said. However unlikely she was in on the murders, if she was, I could be silenced before I told anyone. I should have told her I was going to put the information on Facebook, or call someone right away. I hoped I lived long enough to learn how to be cautious.

I closed my eyes and reassessed. It was unfounded paranoia. Except for dating Paul, I had no real reason to question Judith's integrity.

I called Leslie, anyway. "What do you think about Judith Kimble?"

"She seems like she's serious about getting Gonzo certified as a therapy dog," Leslie said.

"That's not what I'm talking about."

"What then?"

"Do you think she is on the up and up?"

"Up and up? What are you talking about?"

"I talked to her about Paul. She was dating him. She told him about a girl who was inheriting money on her thirteenth birthday. Paul had to know who she was talking about. Do you think Judith is in on the murder? When we were at the nursing home, she suggested that sweet Nurse Blackwell might be The Black One. Do you think she was trying to direct suspicion away from Paul?"

"Why would you think that?"

"Paranoia, I guess."

"You think Judith might be like a double agent or something? Does she know Paul is connected to Carley?"

"I have no idea. I didn't ask."

"I don't think you have anything to worry about, but if your gut says to tread lightly, then be cautious. I don't think you're in danger from Judith."

"I talked to Rocky about my brakes."

"And?"

"He said new brake lines don't come apart. He joked about someone was trying to kill me."

A firm knock on my door made me jump and Truman barked ferociously.

"Someone's at my door. What do I do?" I whispered.

"When someone knocks at the door, you are supposed to answer the door," Leslie said in a singsong voice.

I huffed a hard breath out of my nose. "Smart aleck, you're starting to sound like me."

"That's what friends are for. Go look through the window. Only answer the door if it's a friend. Don't open it for a foe. If you are uncomfortable, I'll stay on the phone."

"A lot of good that will do if someone's here to murder me. Should I hand them the phone so you can yell at them?"

"Now who's the smart aleck?"

I stood on my toes and peaked through the glass crescent at the top of the door. I recognized the hair and opened the door for Jeanine.

"Margie, can you help me with feeding the kids? I sprained my wrist a little and I'm not supposed to use it. Rocky had to leave early." Jeanine waved her bandaged wrist in the air.

"Sure, let me put my boots on. I'll be up there in a second." I closed the door and put the phone to my ear.

"I heard. Go play with the goats." Leslie hung up.

An hour later, the kids were cleaned up, fed, and settled down for a nap. When I got back to my house, the red message light was flashing on my cell phone. The message ID said Judith Kimble. I hesitated, but I punched the play button.

"Hi, Margie. Our conversation made me think back. I remembered one more thing that might be important. I talked to Paul about the folks at the nursing home. I did tell him about Anna talking about murder and The Black One. He seemed surprised at first, then laughed it off. We talked about how older folks are sometimes unclear. I also told him..."

The message cut off. Now what? The logical thing to do was return the call. Not convinced calling was the best thing to do, I cleaned the kitchen and ruminated on the conversation.

Dishes clean and counters wiped, rather than putting off the inevitable I called her back. Judith picked up on the first ring.

"Hi Judith. Thanks for calling. Unfortunately, your message cut off."

Judith repeated the first part of her message. I refocused when she got to the part I had not heard.

"I told Paul about how Mr. Smith agreed Anna was murdered. The funny thing was I didn't bring it up. He asked me if I had heard about Anna, and if anyone believed she was killed. He made light of it. He always degraded folks who are old, calling them deranged and incompetent. He insults people a lot. I hate people who put old folks down. He's a jerk."

"I can vouch for that," I said.

"Their deaths were suspicious. I hope I didn't have anything to do with them passing before their time. I may have. First, I mentioned the girl getting her money. Then I spouted off about Anna saying The Black One caused murders. I should have kept my mouth shut."

"If Paul had anything to do with the murders, you didn't intend to feed him information. I know you didn't want to harm any of the Four Oaks residents."

"No, I never would"

"Do you remember exactly when you told him about Anna talking about The Black One?"

"I'm sure it was the same night I visited Four Oaks with you. Paul and I had dinner together and that is when we talked."

"So your dinner was before Anna and Mr. Smith died?"

"I'm pretty sure it was. I'm not sure which days they died. Why do you think he is connected to their deaths?"

"When I visited Four Oaks by myself, I thought I saw Paul coming out of Anna's room. When I mentioned it to him at Bullard Park, he denied it, but now I am sure it was Paul. He was there right before they found Anna dead. Since I had been there too, it gave the folks at Four Oaks reason to accuse me of Anna's murder. The same happened with Mr. Smith," I said.

"I can't believe I may have been dating a murderer. I'm terrified."

"Unfortunately, I think you were. Keep your doors locked. Thanks for the information."

Judith did not sound like a guilty person, but I was not confident of my character judgment. It would not be the first time I had been duped. As a precaution at future in-person meetings with Judith, I would have someone with me. I had stepped into the world of trust. Betrayal could follow.

Chapter 19

Jerry showed up with two full grocery bags. I questioned whether I was allowing him to fill too much of my life too soon.

He whipped up special dipping sauces while I sliced and breaded zucchini and yellow squash. Jerry guaranteed his special gluten free breadcrumb mix would crisp them perfectly in the oven. He sautéed scallops and shrimp. I poured a couple of glasses of the Chenin Blanc and dinner was ready. We ate on the deck.

"I don't want to dredge up bad thoughts," Jerry said, "but Tara Marshall brought her cat in for its rabies shot today. She asked me to confidentially pass on a bit of information. She said that Ben had talked to that law firm, Hudd and, and whoever else, I can't remember. Anyway, Hudd told him that right before she died, Meredith had her will redone. It directed custody of Carley to him and Tara. They were also named as the trustees of Magdalena Cortosa's estate. In Cortosa's original will, both of Carley's adoptive parents, Olivia and Paul, were named as trustees."

"So originally, Paul was one of the trustees in charge of handling Carley's inheritance as he saw fit?"

"Yes, but Cortosa wasn't naïve, she stipulated that if either parent abandon the girl, the court appointed guardian would become the trustee. Meredith was appointed and she received the power of attorney. She was the only one who had the right to change the will and she did, but only recently."

"But Paul probably didn't know that. Maybe he was banking on the fact that he was named in the original will, and hoping if Carley joined him, he would solidify his claim on the money."

"There's no way to prove he didn't know," Jerry said.

"If Paul didn't know about the new will, but he did know what was in the old will, then there was no reason for him to murder Meredith. Legally, since he was trying to establish a relationship with Carley, he would likely become her guardian and trustee of the estate," I said.

"Hold on. Meredith had changed the will but only recently. It was still with the attorneys for review. She never signed the new will. She died first. When she died, the original was still in effect with Paul receiving control of the estate. I bet he found out about the new will and heard rumors of the stocks' value. In order for him to get his hands on the money, Meredith would have to die before she signed the new will."

"But how could he know about the new will?" I asked.

"I have no idea. Maybe Meredith told him when he showed up to try to claim Carley and whatever money he could."

A shiver ran up my spine. "She was getting better, so she had to be murdered in order for Paul to still be a trustee."

Jerry nodded.

My stomach turned. "Since the new will was not signed does that mean that Paul gets the money?"

"Not if someone can prove he was at Four Oaks and murdered Meredith."

"Let's talk about something else. My head hurts. I need to think about this later," I said.

Jerry chatted about some of his more interesting cases. I asked what Lynn was up to. We shared the goings on of our days. I relaxed.

It was time. "What about Aerosmith?"

Jerry's face changed from relaxed to sorrowful. "Are you sure? It's a heavy hard story."

I wavered for a second. "I think I can handle it."

Jerry was quiet. I knew he was putting together the best way to share what he had to say. I waited, not wanting to pressure him.

"Do you know the lyrics to 'I Don't want to Miss a Thing'?" he asked.

"I know what the song is about, but I can't say I know the lyrics by heart."

"That's good enough. You know it's about loving someone and wanting to be with them forever."

"And ever," I added.

"Yes." He dropped his eyes and stared at the table.

I took a sip of wine, hoping it would fortify me, yet knowing full well that a tablespoon of wine had less alcohol than a big glass of orange juice. I anticipated him saying he had been deeply in love and was dumped. That his heart was broken beyond repair, but he was still in love the woman who dumped him.

"I was married," he began. His voice cracked. "Molly. She was a doctor. A physician. A pediatrician. She had a heart as big as the world." His voice trailed off.

I noticed he spoke in the past tense. I was afraid for him, for what he was going to say next.

"That song was our song. We were very much in love, but Molly was in love with the world, not just me. Her huge heart made me proud to be her husband. She wanted to go to Madagascar and help in the effort to eliminate cholera there."

"I didn't even know cholera was still a problem. I thought it had died out with the development of modern medicine."

Jerry shook his head. "I agreed to go with her, but as a test run she wanted to go first. She wanted to make sure that was what she really wanted to do, before we pulled up all our roots.

"We got married. Our plan was that six months after our wedding, she would go to Madagascar for a month. She got her vaccinations. What she didn't tell me was that she never had her titer checked. She was supposed to do that, but her medical records showed that she never did. Since she was a medical doctor, I assumed that she was doing everything the way she should."

I guessed where he was going. "Maybe she wanted to go there so badly, she didn't want to know."

Jerry's looked perplexed and cocked his head a tiny bit. "I never thought of that. Maybe you're right. You probably guessed the gist of the rest of the story. She went. She was having a great time. Three weeks later, they called me and told me she was ill with cholera. She went downhill so fast. She was in a coma by the time I got there. The doctor working with her said it was a fluke. That for some reason her system was especially vulnerable to the bacterium. The last time I saw her smile was when I took her to the airport to send her off to Madagascar." He hung his head.

"I am so sorry. That must hurt through to your core."

He nodded. "Three years ago and it still wrecks me."

We sat in a comfortable, but emotional silence. I pondered that being widowed was something we had in common. I wondered which pain was worse, losing a spouse you loved or the double hurt of losing a spouse who had rejected your heart. It did not make any difference. We both suffered.

After a few minutes, Jerry lifted his head. "What about you? Have you ever lost a loved one?"

"Yes," I said. Considering the solemnity of the conversation, I should have stopped there, but I did not. "I've lost folks that I loved, but that sure as heck wouldn't include the jerk I was married to."

I whipped the knuckle of my index finger to my mouth and bit it as if that could keep my sarcastic mouth under control. I glanced up in horror.

Jerry raised his eyebrows, and his mouth dropped open. Then he burst out laughing.

I was mortified. "I am so, so sorry," I said.

"What for? One of the things I like about you is that you say what you think. Come on, let's clean up and make dessert. You can explain later."

I dropped my head and shook it, disgusted with my insensitivity.

Jerry reached out his hand, I hesitated then took it, and he pulled me out of the chair. "Come on."

We cleaned up the dinner mess. I recovered from my embarrassment and felt satisfied, but not done. I wanted to continue the evening with Jerry.

I was surprised when he pulled a box of brownie mix out of the last paper bag.

"Don't look shocked," he said. "Sometimes box mix is just as good as from scratch, and it is always easier. It leaves more time to relax. Not everything good has to be fancy and take a lot of effort."

"I told you, I am not complaining about anything anyone cooks for me. You know my limitations, and I see GF on the box, so it works for me." I tapped the box.

Our eyes met and held for a minute. My breaths deepened and quickened without my control.

"Thanks," he said.

"For what?" I asked.

"For giving me the time of day."

My emotional right brain was swirling with all sorts of good feelings, but they refused to translate to my left-brain speech center, so I simply smiled.

He smiled back and tore the top off the box. We made the brownies, then sat close eating them and watched Murdoch Mysteries. We started to nod off, so Jerry went home.

Thoughts about what to do about Paul kept me unsettled and awake. We needed to know if he was the murderer. How could we prove, or disprove it without bringing in the police and casting a bad light on Four Oaks? I would call Leslie in the morning.

Chapter 20

Leslie and I met for lunch and put together what we thought was a foolproof plan. If Paul was a murderer our trap would catch him, but first, we needed to get permission from Four Oaks.

To make sure we were not stepping on anyone's legal rights, we asked Nick to evaluate it. He approved it then called Ms. Hillary and convinced her that considering our plan was in her best interest. We were granted a 30-minute audience to present it.

Armed with overconfidence, Leslie and I headed straight to Four Oaks.

"Where are the dogs?" Sarah asked as Leslie and I signed in.

"At home. Leslie and I have a meeting with Ms. Hillary."

"Her office is over there." Sarah pointed.

"Yes, thank you."

Leslie knocked on the office door.

Ms. Hillary opened it and stepped back. I did not recognize the man sitting in a chair pulled up next to Ms. Hillary's desk.

"Let me introduce you to my friend and Four Oaks board member Mr. Stillwell. He will be listening to your proposal and advising me."

She motioned to the chairs. "Have a seat, you have thirty minutes. Please do not waste it."

Tick tock, tick tock. Sarcasm shot through my brain. '*If you knew Time as well as I do,*' said the Hatter, '*you wouldn't talk about wasting it.*'

I started, "We know who murdered Anna Longmire, Meredith Marshall, and Robert Smith."

"Why do you say they were murdered? Four Oaks considers their deaths natural and the timing coincidental," Ms. Hillary said.

"I know my lawyer Mr. Nick Turner explained the possible consequences if you are wrong," I said.

Ms. Hillary's face dropped.

Leslie continued, "Bear with us. We have a plan that we can keep quiet and out of public scrutiny, but we need to have your permission to put it in place. If the deaths were natural, then there is no harm. No one but a few people will know we even tried it."

"Go on," Mr. Stillwell said.

"If those three residents were murdered, our plan will catch the murderer in another attempt. Four Oaks will receive the recognition. It will show that you care enough about your residents to investigate, even if the police didn't." I was content that I avoided all sarcasm, at least verbally.

"Who are you planning on catching in the act, and what is the plan?" Mr. Stillwell asked.

"We believe Paul Wentworth is the murderer," I said.

"Who is Paul Wentworth?" Ms. Hillary asked.

"He is the ex-son-in-law of Meredith Marshall," Leslie said.

"And what would he have to gain from murdering our residents?" Ms. Hillary scowled.

"Money. Lots of money. Way more money than a fancy Disney sleigh or production cel." I cringed at my sarcastic dig. Would I ever learn?

Ms. Hillary drew back and crinkled her nose indicating she felt my comment stunk.

Leslie glared at me.

I whipped myself back into professional mode. "Sorry, I didn't mean that to sound so harsh. We believe that money was Paul Wentworth's motive, money willed to Mrs. Marshall's granddaughter Carley Marshall. It's a long story, but we'll try to make it clear. You might know part of this already but please listen to what we have found out. I think when you hear how it all fits together you will agree with our plan."

"You'll need to give us some hard evidence," Ms. Hillary said.

Leslie jumped in. "We agree we need hard evidence. Unfortunately, the only things we have are loosely circumstantial. If we had hard evidence, we could call in the police right now. Our theory needs to be tested, and we have a plan for the test. If it works, we will have that hard evidence. And if it doesn't work then there's no harm done."

"And if it does work then we would call the police?" Mr. Stillwell asked.

I continued. "Yes. Here's what we have. Our first assumption is that Mrs. Marshall, Carley's grandmother, was murdered. Mrs. Marshall's daughter was Olivia who was the ex-wife of Paul Wentworth. Olivia and Paul adopted Carley as a newborn."

"Olivia and Paul were Carley's legal parents?" Ms. Hillary asked.

Leslie picked up the explanation. "Yes and no. They legally adopted Carley, but Paul abandoned them when Carley was a toddler. Then Olivia died about five years later and because no one knew where Paul was, Mrs. Marshall ended up with legal custody and power of attorney."

"I'm following you, but I don't see a motive for murder," Ms. Hillary said.

I explained, "Carley's birth mother, Magdalena Cortosa had terminal cancer so she adopted out Carley. She left a will for Carley that was worth millions of dollars in stocks. Paul and Olivia were named trustees."

"You have my attention," Mr. Stillwell said.

Leslie took a turn. "Until Mrs. Marshall got sick, she hadn't considered updating the will. While she was here at Four Oaks, she did have a new will drawn up and it named Ben and his wife Tara as the new trustees until Carley was of age."

"I do remember arranging a meeting with Mrs. Marshall and a lawyer," Ms. Hillary said.

"But if the new will gave the inheritance directly to Carley, there was no reason for Paul to kill anyone," Mr. Stillwell said.

Leslie and I locked eyes for and instant.

Tapping my fingers on the arm of the chair, I explained, "The new will was drawn up, but Meredith had not signed it. We think since she was getting better she didn't feel there was any rush."

Mr. Stillwell nodded. "Common mistake."

Leslie continued, "The only way for Paul to get hold of the stocks was to kill Meredith before she signed the new will and while he was still named the trustee in the original existing will."

I spoke up. "We think his original plan was to get Carley to come live with him, so he would get control of the money without making a scene. But then he found out that Meredith changed the will, and he knew he would be cut out unless Meredith never had the chance to sign the new will."

Ms. Hillary's forehead furrowed and she squeezed her lips together. "Random people from the outside don't know who our residents are or anything about their health. If your theory is true, someone who works here must have known Mrs. Marshall's connection to Paul and provided him up-to-date information about her health."

"Maybe," I said, looking down and tapping my foot.

Ms. Hillary raised her eyebrows high. "Did you tell someone?"

Leslie covered me. "A confidential source told us that Paul knew Mrs. Marshall was recovering."

"Confidential source?" Mr. Stillwell asked.

"We can't tell you who it is right now. Assuming we are right about Paul committing murder, if the information leaked out, our source could be in danger. You need to trust us on this one," I said.

"But how would Paul have known about the new will?" Ms. Hillary asked.

I let out a deep breath. "That's the problem. We don't know for sure that he did. That's one of the reasons we don't want to involve the police yet. We don't want to embarrass you folks at Four Oaks if we are wrong."

Mr. Stillwell drummed his knuckles on the arm of his chair then sat silent for a minute. "How would he know about the large inheritance?"

Leslie explained, "That's another reason we don't want to involve the police at this point. I can only tell you our confidential source admits to inadvertently providing Paul with that information."

"You're giving your confidential source a lot of credibility," Ms. Hillary said, "Why do you think Dr. Anna Longmire and Robert Smith's deaths are connected?"

"They both claimed that Mrs. Marshall was murdered. Paul had to kill them before they convinced someone here that was true. They may have seen him here, Paul may have thought they did," Leslie said.

"Dr. Longmire told us 'The Black One' was the murderer. A friend of ours is Paul's cousin and she said that was a childhood nickname for Paul."

"That sounds plausible, except that I do not believe Mr. Paul Wentworth ever came here to Four Oaks," Ms. Hillary said.

"I'm sure that you don't know all the people who visit here, and it's possible he sneaked in." I could tell by the look on Ms. Hillary's face that she was offended.

"So you want us to take your word that Paul Wentworth obtained confidential information which would inspire him to murder?" Ms. Hillary asked.

Leslie and I slowly nodded in unison.

"I'm not sure your hearsay testimony is enough for us to engage in some drastic plan. What exactly are the details of this plan of yours?" Mr. Stillwell asked.

"We want to set a trap," Leslie said.

"A trap, like a bear trap, or maybe a jungle rope trap? Nonsense! Setting a trap of any sort sounds woefully illegal," Ms. Hillary said with a smirk.

I focused on my feet, took a breath, then looked up. "Actually, it's a set up. We bait Paul Wentworth with information that would compel him to murder someone else. We catch him in the act when he tries."

"Are you police trained?" Mr. Stillwell asked.

Leslie leaned forward. "No, but if Paul is the murderer, he does not use weapons. He wants the deaths to look natural. All we need is one person bigger than Paul to slow him down. We can get a bunch of others to hold him in the room until the police get here," Leslie said.

"What if he gets violent?" Mr. Stillwell asked.

"Then we sit on him, or if need be, we let him go. We will have the evidence we need, and it will be a detective's job to track him down. All we need to show is that he tried to murder one more person who was connected to the others' deaths. That is enough to get him arrested and we can help the police by providing our evidence."

"You really have nothing other than a childhood nickname, and hearsay from an unnamed source to connect him to the murders. Wanting money and trying to gain custody of one's daughter are not motives for murder. We do need solid evidence," Ms. Hillary said. Her back stiffened more, if that was possible.

"I understand. Everything combined seriously points toward Paul Wentworth as the murderer. Especially since he has no friends or family to visit here. If he takes the bait and simply shows up, it is suspicious. I am sure the police can connect all the dots," Leslie said.

I questioned if Ms. Hillary's apparent caution was really an attempt to protect her own involvement. The longer she hesitated, the more my suspicions grew. If she would not help us, I was not sure what to do, but I would be convinced that she was in on the murders in some way.

It was then that I noticed a small photo on her credenza that gave me chills. It was a photo of a Welsh Corgi. I told myself that a lot of people besides Paul Wentworth had Welsh Corgis. I had sense enough not to ask about it, right then.

In spite of my reservations, I had to give one last try. "I have a simple request. It won't take much time or energy and won't intrude on anyone's privacy. If Paul was here the days of the murders, it ties everything together in a neat package. Can we take a look at Sarah's sign-in book to see if Paul signed in on the days Mrs. Marshall, Dr. Longmire, and Mr. Smith died?"

"That sounds reasonable," Mr. Stillwell said.

Ms. Hillary squirmed in her seat. "I don't want anyone from the outside digging through our records. We can look for his signature and discuss whether or not we want to hear your plan. Come back tomorrow and we'll give you an answer."

"Thank you. We have a therapy dog visit scheduled here for tomorrow," I said. *And unfortunately, your delay provides plenty of time for you to tamper with the evidence.*

Leslie and I excused ourselves.

"Why do you think she is dragging her feet?" I asked as we headed out the door to our cars.

"She strikes me as the kind of person who is fearful of embracing new ideas. She doesn't want anything to disrupt her perceived sphere of control."

"Maybe, but it makes me suspicious. What if those two are in on it? We just set ourselves up for who knows what. The next thing you know, I'll be waking up with a goat head in my bed or something worse."

"I don't think so, and it was a horse head," Leslie said.

"Goats are easier and more plentiful where I live. What makes you so sure Hillary and Stillwell aren't involved?"

"Gut feeling."

"Well, now I have total confidence in the world around me."

Leslie threw up her hands mocking surprise, "I'm so glad!"

I measured Ms. Hillary's reluctance against Leslie's gut feeling. I hoped Leslie's gut was right.

Chapter 21

Truman and Rusta bounced around like unruly puppies in the field next to Four Oaks. We hoped the romp would relieve excess energy. The last thing we needed was for them to cut up in Ms. Hillary's office. We wiped their paws and went in to face Ms. Hillary and Mr. Stillwell.

Her door was open, so I knocked on the frame to announce our arrival. She beckoned us in. Leslie and I headed to the chairs and Truman playfully grabbed Rusta's back leg holding on with a soft-mouth play bite. His jaw clamped on her leg without pressure. Rusta swung around and nipped Truman's side and they spun in a circle. Disgraced, Leslie and I grabbed their collars and pulled them apart.

"I'm so sorry," I said. "We let them play outside, and I guess they weren't finished."

Leslie pushed down on Rusta's butt, trying to make the dog sit. Rusta bounced her rear up and down like a hopping rabbit.

"Give us a minute to organize them."

Mr. Stillwell and Ms. Hillary watched, their gazes burning through me.

I pulled my chair a little further away from Leslie's. We finally got the dogs to lay down on the far sides of our chairs. "I'm so sorry. They really are good dogs, but they do have minds of their own."

"I see," Ms. Hillary said.

Mr. Stillwell moved to close the door to Ms. Hillary's office. As Mr. Stillwell walked by, Truman barely moved his head to capture a whiff of feet. I was relieved he had morphed back into therapy dog mode and stayed still.

Ms. Hillary folded her hands and placed them on her desk. "Mr. Stillwell and I spent a lot of time reviewing the Four Oaks visitor sign-in ledger."

Just call it Sarah's Sign-in like everyone else.

She put her cup to her lips and sipped whatever was in her cup. "I'm so sorry. How rude of me. I was distracted by the antics of your dogs. Would you like coffee, or maybe some tea?" she asked.

Just get on with it, PLEASE. "No thank you," I said.

"I would love some coffee," Leslie said.

I refrained from rolling my eyes at her.

"I'll get it for you. Creamer, sugar?" Mr. Stillwell offered.

"Two plain creamers, please."

This is going to take forever.

Mr. Stillwell headed toward Leslie, the steaming cup filled to overflow. He passed Rusta. My mind jumped to - dog jumps up - hot coffee spilled on Ms. Hillary's office carpet - meeting called off until carpet is cleaned - I would go to my grave wondering if Paul had signed the ledger.

Hallelujah, he made it. My breath whooshed out of my lungs. I wasn't aware I had been holding it.

Mr. Stillwell returned to his chair. "I'm sorry, but we couldn't find any signatures that clearly read as Mr. Wentworth's."

I was stunned. I had been so sure. "Not even one? Could he have sneaked in?"

Ms. Hillary's cheek twitched. "Our security here is nearly impenetrable. However, we did find one signature that I didn't recognize. It was in the book on each of the three days in question, the days that Mrs.

Marshall, Dr. Longmire, and Mr. Smith died. Of course yours and other regular visitors' were there too."

"What name didn't you recognize?" I asked.

"John Preston," Mr. Stillwell said.

"Who is that?" Leslie asked.

"We have no idea. We asked Sarah and she said the license matched the signature. Her mind is like video recording."

"Did you ask her for a description of the man?" I asked.

"You may be aware of Sarah's unique skill in recognizing and remembering signatures and recalling faces and details. We did ask, and she remembered. He was medium build, dark brown hair, and greenish eyes. His driver's license was from New Jersey. She doesn't remember any conversation with him, which is not unusual."

"That description sounds like it could be Paul Wentworth," I said. "Could it be a fake license?"

Mr. Stillwell answered. "We discussed that possibility. We don't see many New Jersey licenses here, so it's possible that Sarah wouldn't recognize a forgery."

"So are you interested in putting our plan in place?" I asked cautiously.

"We are interested in hearing exactly what you have planned. We want every detail from start to finish."

Anna, Meredith, Mr. Smith, your deaths will be avenged!

"Thank you," I said but wanted to get up and dance.

Leslie and I rolled out the plot for the trap. Mr. Stillwell and Ms. Hillary sat and listened without interrupting. We finished. Mr. Stillwell and

Ms. Hillary sat quietly. Leslie and I stroked our dogs to keep our blood pressure from skyrocketing.

Mr. Stillwell broke the silence. "So first, you want to talk to Bart Whitehead? Is that correct?"

"Yes," I said.

"Ms. Hillary, does Mr. Whitehead have any relatives that we should consult?" Mr. Stillwell asked.

"He was self admitted through his physician. I don't recall the involvement of any relatives."

"And he seems of sound mind?"

"Yes, he is," Ms. Hillary answered.

"Do you see any problems with us involving Mr. Whitehead?" Mr. Stillwell asked.

"No. But the conversation needs to be here in my office. It will be best if he agrees with all of us present. That way I can be assured we are all on the same page. Mr. Stillwell and I to discuss this with Mr. Whitehead prior to giving you ladies the go ahead."

Obviously, you can't make any decisions on the spot. I hope you never have any emergencies. "That sounds best," I said.

"I assume you are planning on doing your volunteer dog visit today," Ms. Hillary said, motioning toward Truman and Rusta. "Please let us have about 30 minutes and then drop back by."

"Will do," I said.

"And if you visit Bart Whitehead, make it a regular therapy dog visit. Do NOT mention anything to him. "

"I promise we won't," Leslie said. We headed out the door to do comfort visits.

"Bart Whitehead first?" Leslie asked as soon as we were out the door.

"Why not? We need to determine if he is mentally sound enough to participate."

Leslie rolled her eyes.

Bart was in his room sitting in front of the TV. He did not look like the spunky man I had seen talking to Mr. Smith a few days ago.

"Bart? Can Rusta and Truman come say hello to you?" I asked.

He waved us in, his eyes on the TV.

Truman went to one side of his wheelchair and Rusta to the other. Bart put a hand on each dog's head then back in his lap.

"Bart, you don't seem to be feeling well."

He glared at me. "No."

"Is there something I can do to help?"

"Can you bring people back to life?"

"No. Sometimes I wish I could. It sounds like you are missing someone."

He sat still. Truman nudged Bart's arm with his nose. Bart did not respond. Truman nudged again, flipping Bart's arm up a little. Bart raised his hand.

I questioned his next move, not sure if he would push Truman away or pet him.

"Bob. I miss Bob." He stroked Truman down the back of his neck.

"Robert Smith?" Leslie asked.

Bart nodded and tears filled his eyes. He reached out his other hand and stroked Rusta.

"I'm sorry. You two hit it off pretty well," I said.

He nodded again. "He wasn't supposed to die."

Here we go again. Death by nature or death unnatural?

"It is hard," Leslie joined in.

"I came here because I was so lonely at my house. I couldn't get out and enjoy company. The only people I ever saw were the delivery folks. When I came here, I felt almost young again. Bob told me the folks around here were getting murdered. As a former detective, I thought he was exaggerating, but now I wonder if I'm next. The office folks here aren't doing a thing about it. I'm sitting here waiting for the grim reaper to come harvest me. I didn't know Bob long, but he gave me hope. Now my hope is gone."

Leslie nodded.

I knelt down beside him. "Bart, there is hope. I can't tell you anything, but trust me something will be done."

His eyes searched my face. He started to say something.

I held my finger in front of my lips. "Shh. Not yet. I can't talk about it."

The corner of Bart's mouth twitched, not quite a half-smile. He scratched the dogs vigorously on their necks.

On the way to the next room, Leslie let out a huge breath. "That was intense."

"I wanted to tell him so badly."

"Me, too. I hope they don't dawdle on this! Bart is so depressed. He might go downhill fast."

"I agree. I bet he will be willing to do whatever we need him to do."

"Yeppers," Leslie said.

We stopped at the activity room. Five residents watched Truman's repertoire of tricks. The dog would do anything for a piece of freeze-dried liver. The residents clapped and we excused ourselves. Ms. Hillary was waiting outside the door.

"Can you come back to my office?" She asked.

I glanced down the hallway and saw Mr. Stillwell wheeling Bart out of his room.

"Sure," we both said.

Bart noticed us talking with Ms. Hillary. He raised his eyebrows and grinned.

"Mr. Whitehead is more chipper since you visited him," Ms. Hillary said, her lips pursed and forehead wrinkled.

"He loves our dogs. That's why we come here," Leslie said.

I kept my mouth shut.

We followed Mr. Stillwell and Bart into the office. Ms. Hillary closed the door behind her.

"Mr. Whitehead, is it correct that you were friends with Robert Smith?" Mr. Stillwell asked.

"Yes, and before you ask, yes, I think he was murdered. That's what you wanted to ask isn't it? You're trying to figure out if this crazy old man here," he pointed to his chest, "is tarnishing the reputation of your marvelous old folks' home."

"Not exactly. You were a detective and we respect your opinion in this matter," Ms. Hillary said.

Mr. Stillwell continued, "We agree there might be a possibility that someone here was murdered."

"Well for god's sake call the police," Bart said, crossing his arms over his chest.

"There isn't enough to accuse someone, and we want to keep this low key until we do," Mr. Stillwell said.

I rolled my eyes.

Bart squinted one eye as if it helped him to think. "So you need more evidence?"

"Precisely," Ms. Hillary said.

"You want to do a set up?" Bart asked.

"We are considering it. But if we are dealing with a murderer, it will be extremely dangerous for you. You would be the bait."

"Your security cameras can record it," Bart said.

"We have visual monitoring devices in the hallways, but we don't have them in the residents' rooms. That would violate privacy. In order to bait a murderer, you will have to be somewhere that is isolated from the rest of the residents. You will need to be in your room alone, where we don't have cameras," Mr. Stillwell said.

"But I can use my own camera." Bart pulled his cell phone from a pocket in his wheelchair. "I can do a video call and accidentally leave it on, and put in on my night stand facing the door. It will show the intruder as he enters the door."

"But he will see the phone is on," I said.

"Not if I cover the screen. It's my room, my phone and I can be as kinky as I want."

"We try to dissuade kinky here," Ms. Hillary said.

"Well give me a gun, then," Bart said.

"Out of the question," Mr. Stillwell said.

"Of course," Bart said. "However you need me to help, say it. I can be bait if that's what you need. If someone killed Bob and his friends, then I want to be in on the take down. I don't care if I'm killed in the process. I would be glad to go down in a blaze of glory to avenge my friend. It's a better way to go than deteriorating in this chair." Bart shook the arms of his wheelchair.

"Thank you, Mr. Whitehead. We will likely take you up on your offer. First, we need to put a few other pieces in place, but if all of those work out, we will need your help."

"Woooo wooo," Bart whistled and a huge smile spread across his face. "I'm back in the saddle again!"

Chapter 22

I was elected to set the next piece of the trap in motion. I had to talk to Judith. I arranged for her to bring her dog and meet Leslie, me and our dogs for coffee at Can-Con. Priorities ruled and we made sure the dogs were friendly and comfortable playing before we ordered coffee and sat down to chat.

"Judith, we desperately need your help," I said.

"Pawty doggie event?" she asked.

"No, and I'm not sure you are going to like what I have to ask."

She eyed me over the rim of her cup and sipped. "Go ahead, ask."

"We need you to talk to Paul."

Judith choked on the coffee she was swallowing. "What? Why? That sounds nasty."

"Do you remember when we talked about the Paul, Meredith, and Carley connection?"

She nodded.

"Some folks at the nursing home said that they thought Meredith was murdered."

"Like Anna and Mr. Smith?"

"Yes. It seems to be more than a coincidence that after you told Paul they suspected murder, they died too. They may have been murdered, but since they were old and somewhat fragile, it's a bit hard to tell."

Judith put her cup down and started clicking her nails. "Are you telling me you think Paul was getting information from me and then killing off people to keep the truth from getting out?"

"Yes," Leslie said quietly.

"Son of a b." Judith made a fist and hit the table. A little of my coffee splashed out of the cup.

"I told you that you wouldn't like it." She convinced me she was no longer Paul's friend.

"I hate it," Judith said.

"There isn't enough evidence to convince the cops they should arrest him, so we want to set him up," Leslie said.

"And you need me to help? You want me to talk to him. Gross."

"But will you do it?" I asked.

Judith scrunched her face. "What do you need me to do?"

"We need you to meet with Paul. Tell him Bart Whitehead, a resident at Four Oaks, is saying the deaths were murders, and they are all connected. Also, casually mention that I was arrested for the murders but released. Tell him you were supposed to go with me to visit Four Oaks tomorrow, but you are suspicious that I am the murderer, so you aren't going. Tell him you are afraid I might kill someone else."

"That sounds good, but I heard through the grape vine Paul is moving out of town, the day after tomorrow," Judith said.

"Figures! Call him today and ask him out tonight for a farewell dinner. Tell him you will make it special," I said.

"He'll ruin my appetite, but I'll do it, and believe me, setting him up will be special for me."

"Let us know when you have accomplished your mission."

"Sir, yes, sir," Judith saluted.

"Tempus fugit," I said.

"I think that's Semper fi," Leslie said.

"No, I meant time is flying," I said.

"Carpe diem," Judith said and held up her cup for us to toast.

Satisfied, I went home. Savoring solitude, I sipped tea on my deck and listened to the birds singing. Less than five minutes had passed when my phone rang.

Jerry's voice was cheery. "How's it going? Are you up to anything tonight?"

I was caught with a hand in the candy jar. "Sort of."

"Does that mean I can't bring a bottle of wine by to share with you?"

"A glass of good wine sounds terrific."

"Can I pick up sandwiches from The Sandwich Earl? I'm at the clinic until six."

"Pimento cheese on gluten-free with side of their tomato chunk salad."

"What's the proper wine to pair with pimento cheese sandwiches?"

I rolled my eyes. "How about a bottle of Screaming Eagle Cabernet Sauvignon 1992?" I asked, referring to a premium wine costing over $4,000 a bottle.

"Um—no, but I will find a somewhat reasonable facsimile."

"If you must." I enjoyed sparring with Jerry.

He arrived a few hours later, wine and sandwiches in hand. The evening was comfortably cool, so we sat on the deck surrounded by citron candles. The atmosphere had purpose.

"How was your day?" I asked, delaying telling Jerry about tomorrow's plans.

He told me about a 30-pound Maine Coon cat with a proportionately huge hairball, a bull terrier with an OCD spinning disorder, and a Jack Russell that broke its toe chasing a rabbit.

"You'd be out of business without those flashing Jacks."

"Don't you know it. How about your day?"

The delay was over. I had to explain. "We are setting a trap."

"Who is setting a trap for what?"

"For Paul, at Four Oaks."

"I'm glad the police finally decided to get involved," Jerry said.

"That's the thing. They didn't"

"Then who is doing the trapping?"

"Ms. Hillary didn't want to involve the police yet. She doesn't want undue bad publicity. The police won't touch it because we don't have one piece of connecting evidence. They had to drop charges on me for lack of evidence. Also, there's no possibility of exhuming Anna or Meredith, and Mr. Smith was cremated."

"You are avoiding the question. Who is doing the trapping?"

"Ms. Hillary is in charge."

Jerry cocked his head, pulled his chin down and eyed me over his glasses. "Ms. Hillary? I gather she came around? This does not sound like a great idea. I sense an oncoming mega-muck up."

"I think it will be okay. Either Paul shows or he doesn't. We don't actually have to catch him, just catch him in the act."

"And he is going to say, 'you got me, I give up?'"

"If he doesn't, Four Oaks has surveillance cameras in the halls and Bart's cell phone will be set up in his room."

"Who is Bart?"

"He's the retired detective who was Mr. Smith's friend."

"So you have a geriatric detective trying to subdue an athletic male in his prime? What could go wrong?" Jerry shook his head.

"We have Juan helping us too."

"Juan?"

"He's an ex-gang member who works at Four Oaks."

"Why does this not sound like one of the world's ten best ideas?" Jerry asked.

"It does sound a bit flaky, but I am sure it will work."

My phone dinged an incoming text. It was Judith. "Plan in place. He took the bait like a starving fish." Happy face emoji.

I texted back, "He will flounder!" Fish emoji.

Judith texted back six laughing-with-tears emojis.

Jerry glared at me.

"Part one of the plan is already in effect. The perp has taken the bait. We are on for tomorrow."

Jerry put his hand on mine sending my stomach into knots. I suppressed a gasp and coughed to relieve the tension in my throat.

"I'm worried about you. Do you have to go? Can't you let them deal with it?"

"Unfortunately, I have to show up so Paul thinks he can pin Bart's death on me."

"If he kills Bart and gets away with it, you might be blamed."

"Then I guess we can't let Bart be killed."

"And what if Paul doesn't show?"

"Then I admit I'm wrong."

"Or maybe someone else is the killer. Be careful, please." He squeezed my hand.

"I'll have Truman with me," I said.

"I'm not sure he will be able to protect you."

"But I'm sure I will protect him with my life. If someone will murder a human, they wouldn't mind hurting a dog. I won't put Truman in harm's way. I'll be careful."

"Didn't you say there was a nurse there you also suspected. Does she know about the plan?"

"I don't think so, but it shouldn't make any difference."

"It may not make any difference at the nursing home, but if Paul isn't your man, you might be next on someone else's list."

"Such a pleasant note to end the evening on."

"You're playing with fire."

"And I intend for someone to get burned, but not me." If our relationship was meant to grow, Jerry had to face and accept the real person of Margie Vonn.

"Do me one favor. Keep me posted via text."

"Will do."

Chapter 23

I pulled into the parking lot and saw Leslie walking Rusta on the side of the Four Oaks building.

I leashed Truman and headed straight toward her.

"What are you doing here?" I asked. "This was supposed to be me only."

"Are you getting territorial with therapy dog visits?" Leslie asked.

"You know this is not a real visit."

"It will look more normal if I'm here with you. It's rare when we visit alone. Besides, you can use someone to watch your back."

I blew out a hard breath. "You have a point. Just be sure you act normally."

We signed Sarah's log and beelined to Ms. Hillary's office.

"I was under the assumption only Margie and Truman would be here," Ms. Hillary said, glancing toward Mr. Stillwell who was pouring coffee.

"So did I, but Leslie has a point that two of us looks normal."

Mr. Stillwell sat down. "The big problem is that Paul was expecting Margie to be alone. If you are with her, then you would be a witness who could state that Margie is not in on the murder."

Leslie shook her head. "Oh no, I didn't think of that. Can I hide out here? Rusta and I can sit where no one can see us from the hallway. If something goes wrong, it would be better to have more boots on the ground."

Ms. Hillary pointed to the left side of her office where a door was standing ajar. "You can sit in there with us as long as your dog behaves."

Through the opening in the doorway, I saw several monitors that displayed live images of the hallways and entries at Four Oaks.

"Cool," Leslie said, "that will work."

"You have monitors! Do you store all your recordings, or do you have the kind that cycle and overwrite?" I asked.

"I cannot discuss our security with you." Ms. Hillary nodded her head toward the clock on her wall. "It's time. This is when you are expected to start your visit."

Mr. Stillwell stood up, threw his shoulders back, and cleared his throat. In his deepest voice, he said, "Let's make sure we are all on the same page. Margie, you will do your regular visits to our residents' rooms. The three of us will monitor the cameras. If we see Paul Wentworth enter the building, Ms. Hillary will text you."

"Got it," I said.

Mr. Stillwell continued, "When you receive Ms. Hillary's text, you will go hang out near Bart's room until you see Paul heading that way. You will pretend you don't see Paul, but when you know he notices you, you'll enter Bart's room."

Like I was planning on waving and giving him a hug. I was going to interrupt and tell him I was not ignorant, but decided against it.

Mr. Stillwell's voice slowed to a deliberate cadence. "You will visit for only a few seconds. Bart will act like he is asleep. When you are in Bart's room you will tell him to start his camera. His phone is on the dresser and he has a remote control under the covers. After a few seconds, leave Bart's room and head to another room, away from Paul, still pretending you didn't see him. We will watch on the monitors until Paul goes into the room. Then we will tie up this mess."

Ms. Hillary straightened her glasses. "If Mr. Paul Wentworth doesn't show up, you will continue visiting as you always do. We will keep surveillance of the hallways. After you finished visiting, both dog teams will leave. If he doesn't show up for two hours after you leave. We call it off."

And if Paul doesn't show up here, then I will likely end up dead meat somewhere else at some other time. I am sure he is the murderer.

Roaming the halls, I began visiting as always. Truman's face was pinched and his ears drooped. His head notched to the side, he made eye contact with me asking in dog language, "what's wrong?" I never could fool that dog. He knew when I was tense. I gave him extra treats in an effort to redirect his attention away from me. We went up and down the halls visiting folks who were awake and even visited some rooms twice.

I was about to give up and leave when at I saw someone I thought was Paul at the far end of the hallway. He was standing by the drink machine, with his back toward me. I was almost certain it was Paul. How could he make it so deep inside Four Oaks and no one texted me to let me know? A shiver went down my spine. Was he there to assist someone else in a murder, the murder of me?

I touched my phone. I had muted my phone when we were in the meeting earlier. I whipped it out of my bag and of course there were two messages. The first said, "Wentworth is signing in." The second was much more ominous. It said, "Signed in as John Preston."

My stomach lurched. I wished part of the plan had been to alert the police. Too late now, we could never get a second chance.

I headed to Bart's room as planned. I hoped Paul was watching. There was no way I could turn around and look. I opened Bart's door and took a half step forward. With the heavy shades drawn down, the room was dark. I could see a tiny light on the cell phone on the nightstand but would not have noticed it if I had not been looking for it. The phone screen was blacked out as planned. I hoped Bart's phone could catch some video in the low light. At least it would catch the opening and closing of the door. The only other thing I could make out was a pile of blankets in the chair by the window and a lump in the bed that I assumed was Bart.

"He's here. Start your camera," I whispered.

A thumbs up popped out from under the lump in the bed and then ducked back under. I hoped the old man had whatever it took to go through with this.

I backed out of the room like I always did when I discovered a resident was asleep. I headed down the hallway in the opposite direction from the drink machine. Opening the next door, I slipped into Mrs. Hancock's room for the third time that day. Through a crack in the door I saw Paul was heading up the hallway toward Bart's room.

"What are you looking at dear?" Mrs. Hancock's voice startled me.

"Oh, just someone I know."

"Must be someone that you want to hide from."

Why are old folks sharp and on the mark just when you want them to be off in their own world?

I peeked out the door but didn't see Paul. A loud thump reverberated from inside Bart's closed door. Ms. Hillary and Mr. Stillwell were flying down the hallway. Leslie followed. Rusta was bouncing up and down, trying to pull the leash out of Leslie's hand. Every other bounce, Rusta emitted a muted woof.

Mrs. Hancock shrieked as I threw open her door and headed toward Bart's room. The sound of a chair hitting the floor inside made me briefly debate opening Bart's door, but Mr. Stillwell beat me to it. He grabbed the handle, shoved it open and flipped on the light. The blankets that had been in the chair were in a heap on the floor. Juan had Paul pinned down on top of them. Paul flailed his legs and rocked back and forth trying to free his arms. Bart swung a cane over their heads, but Juan's head blocked Bart's swing.

"Did someone call 911?" I yelled.

"Yes!" Ms. Hillary answered, running into the room. She hopped around the struggling men.

The woman has some great footwork. I told my brain to shut up. This was not a time to be sarcastic.

Juan's wrestling moves were typical street brawl as opposed to law enforcement tactical moves. Paul lurched and Juan flew off. Paul pushed up on his knees. Bart raised his cane and whacked Paul on the side of the head. Paul grabbed the cane and threw it at Bart. It winged Bart's arm. Bart sat back hard on his bed. Paul ran for the door. Truman and I blocked the doorway.

Truman jumped in front of me, lowered his head and bared his teeth. I had never seen him threaten anyone like that. Paul slowed down enough so when he drew back to kick Truman, Juan tackled him. Truman's barks indicated he wanted to shred Paul.

A fragile resident pushed me from behind. I stood my ground.

"MOVE!" Renee Blackwell shouted, as she negotiated a lowered gurney through a group of elders who had gathered to watch the fracas.

Once in the room, she pointed to Ms. Hillary and Mr. Stillwell and yelled, "legs". They each grabbed the closest leg while she and Juan each grabbed an arm. They pushed Paul backwards onto the gurney. Paul continued thrashing, but Mr. Stillwell put his knee on one of Paul's legs then strapped it to the gurney. Then he strapped down the leg Ms. Hillary was holding. Together they strapped down his arms. Paul fought against the restraints, but they held.

Sirens shrieking, altered us the police arrived. The officers rushed past Sarah who was faithfully manning her sign-in station. They rushed into Bart's room to find Paul trussed up like a turkey.

"I broke a nail," Ms. Hillary whined. Her hair was disheveled, but her smile was huge.

Four officers checked Paul's restraints and two others stood guard at the door to ward off curious residents. Sitting on his bed, Bart waved to the folks peeping in the door.

I plopped in the chair and hugged Truman close to my leg. I needed doggie therapy. He obliged by putting his head on my lap. I drew a couple of deep breaths and let them out, counting to five. One of the policemen guarding the door reached out an arm blocking a confused oldster from entering the room. Several more residents jostled for a glimpse inside the room.

I marveled at the possibilities of news headlines. *"Two Buff Cops Fend Off 6 Elders Whose Combined Ages Totaled 550 Years."* Or maybe a headline with a focus on Bart, *"Senile Senior Snares Slayer."* Or an unbiased descriptor, *"Attempted Murder on Dying Man."* My sarcasm brain was working. I was okay.

Two aides herded the residents into the dining room at a pace slower than a lame three-toed sloth. Paul cooperated as they took him away. After being tricked by a decrepit detective, I imagined Paul's ego was more bruised than his body. I was proud Peaceful Pets helped collar the perp. It was a good day's work at the quiet nursing home.

I was texting Jerry when Leslie and Rusta walked up.

"Great job! Let's go get a cuppa at Can-Con. My treat," Leslie said.

"I need to go to the police station and give a statement, first. I'm sure they will want yours if you were watching on the video screen."

"I was. It was so exciting!"

"Cuppa at Can-Con after?"

"That would be perfect. Let me tell Bart I'll be back for a real visit tomorrow. Can you text Judith and invite her to meet with us? I'm sure she would like to hear all the thrilling details."

"I don't have Judith's number."

"Not a problem. She has called me. I have the number. I'll text her."

In my car, I texted Judith's number. The text bounced back. I headed for the police station. I would try again when I got there.

Chapter 24

I parked at the police station and texted Judith again. The message failed again. I scrolled down the recent calls on my phone and tapped the call button by Judith's name. The call went straight to voice mail so I left a message.

The police interview lasted for half an hour. When I was done, I tried Judith's number again, but again it went to voicemail.

Leslie and I headed to Can-Con. The parking lot was full with only four empty spaces. "What's up with all the cars? I have never seen the lot so full," I asked.

Leslie shrugged. "I don't know. Maybe there's a dog club meeting here."

"I recognize some of the cars. They're Peaceful Pets members. See the stickers on their windows?"

Leslie nodded. "Let's go check it out."

The sliding glass doors slid open, and Truman and Rusta lunged into their favorite store. Not far on the other side of the door, about half our Peaceful Pets members stood with their dogs.

"Did we miss a meeting announcement?" I asked.

Charlotte ran up to me, Inky pouched in the bag hanging at her side. She gave me a chest-busting hug. "We are so proud of you. You didn't give up and you made the world a safer place."

"Thanks, but..."

Charlotte grabbed my hand and spun me toward the coffee bar next to doggie playground. "Let me buy you a cup of coffee. We all want to hear about it." Her Vanna White arm sweep included all the club members.

Oh great. Now Charlotte wants me to ruin the case by talking too much.

Except for inky, we turned our dogs out into the doggie playground, and Truman and Rusta took off for the water feature. The women shoved together three tables, and ordered coffee.

"Ladies, I appreciate your interest, but I'm not sure how much I can talk about it. The last thing I want to do is jeopardize the case," I said.

A collective depressive 'oh' came from around the table.

"But I can tell you what happened in Bart's room. A lot of people saw what happened there."

Enthusiastic 'ahs' replaced the 'ohs'.

"Before I do that, does anyone know where Judith and Gonzo are?"

All heads shook no.

"The police called the shelter to pick up Paul's dogs. A girl from the shelter picked them up and told us Gonzo wasn't with the others," Charlotte said.

"Does anyone have Judith's address?"

"Peggy, but she's not here."

"Can someone text Peggy and get Judith's address? I'm worried about her."

"I can," Charlotte said.

We drank coffee and I fed my story to hungry ears. The ladies giggled and groaned, encouraging me to embellish the details. Leslie shared what she saw from her vantage point, until everyone seemed to be satisfied.

"What's going to happen to Paul's dogs?" Leslie asked.

Charlotte stuck her chin out and sniffed. "Ingrid said she will take care of them."

"Ingrid?" I groaned.

"Yes. She may not be the nicest to people, but her dogs live in dog-heaven."

"If you say so. But if I die and come back as a dog, please don't make her my owner."

Coffee droplet giggles spurted from some of the members.

My phone dinged. It was a text from Jerry. "Dinner tomorrow, your place, me cook?"

"YES!"

The hoopla subsided and I headed home. When I opened the car door, my joints resisted movement indicating I was headed for another flare. I slated a night of relaxation and disassociation from the real world.

I threw Truman's leash on the kitchen counter, poured a glass of wine and retreated to my TV chair. The doorbell rang.

This better be Santa Claus or Jesus returning because nothing else is worth my getting out of this chair.

Jerry was on the porch holding a Chinese takeout bag. "Can I come in? We don't have to talk."

"Of course and thank you. I thought you were coming tomorrow."

"I am. I'm cooking for you tomorrow. Tonight is take-it-easy take out."

"Works for me. But only if we can watch TV while we eat. I'm talked out"

"Fine. But I do have something I need to talk to you about. That's why I dropped in tonight."

"Please tell me it isn't something ominous."

"Not too."

I grabbed some plates and we set up a buffet on the coffee table. I turned the TV to PBS.

"What do you need to talk to me about?"

Jerry took in a deep breath.

"You remember Nick? The lawyer who helped get you out of jail?"

"Of course."

"He took on Paul Wentworth's case."

I stuffed a piece of avocado roll sushi in my mouth. The wasabi burned more than I expected.

"I guess I won't be using Nick for a lawyer again."

"Since he's a criminal lawyer, I would hope not."

"If he was a Facebook friend, I would unfriend him."

Jerry chuckled. "I understand."

"Can you ask him something for me?"

"What's that?"

"Can you find out if he knows anything about Judith? I've been trying to contact her all afternoon. She doesn't answer. Since she was involved with Paul, I'm worried about her."

"Sure."

Jerry texted Nick, "Do you know anything about Judith Kimble?"

Jerry's phone dinged a message fifteen minutes into the Antiques Road show.

"He says, 'No comment.'"

"What does that mean?" I asked.

"It means because of lawyer client privilege he can't say anything. If he didn't know anything, he would probably say so."

"Ask him if Judith is okay."

Jerry texted again and another no comment message dinged on his phone.

"Does that mean Paul killed Judith?" I asked.

"It could mean a lot of things."

"I hate this, not knowing."

"If Judith is dead, it won't be public information until after the police notify next of kin."

"Can you drop by his office and talk to Nick? Maybe he doesn't want to say anything that can be documented. Texts are written record."

"Will do."

"I almost wish I hadn't gotten her mixed up in this."

We watched TV in compatible silence until my eyes drooped. When Jerry left, he gave me a friendly hug.

I wanted this Four Oaks episode to be over and move on to something else. I plopped in bed, and stroking Caravaggio's head I soothed myself to sleep. If sleep was the word for what I did that night.

Chapter 25

The pressure from Caravaggio sitting on my chest and drooling woke me up. I shooed him away. My mouth was dry, my joints hurt and I was more tired than when I went to bed. I lay flat on my back for half an hour clearing my mind.

Truman put his front paws on the bed and nudged my arm with his nose. I hauled my sorry buns out of bed. Flare be damned, life beckoned. I had a hungry dog and I had promised Bart I would visit.

As I pulled in the parking lot at Four Oaks, I anticipated another cheering welcome party and was glad when there was none. I was exhausted, so Bart might be the only resident I visited.

I walked in the door and Sarah stood up and reached out her hand to shake mine. Surprised by her unusual behavior, I drew back an instant then obliged and put my hand out. Her handshake crunched my aching knuckles.

"Nice job! Thank you," she said. She stroked Truman on his back.

My heart sang.

I glanced into Ms. Hillary's office as I walked by. She was concentrating on whatever she was typing on her computer. Down the hall, in one of the social areas, a group of eight seniors surrounded Bart.

I caught the end of what he was saying.

"...and when he put the pillow on my head," Bart mimed a pillow being flattened on his face, " Juan leaped out from under the blankets," he threw his arms in the air, "and tore the creep off of me," he grabbed fists of air and yanked.

The seniors clapped.

"Margie! Welcome. Meet my friends." Bart waved his arm in a circle over his head.

Truman visited each senior in turn, collecting compliments, pats and neck scratches.

"Good dog."

"Better than Rin-Tin-Tin."

"The heart of Lassie."

"So all is well here?" I asked Bart.

"Wonderful. I'm meeting new folks and everyone wants to hear the story."

"Do you think you'll get tired of telling it?"

"Maybe. See that guy over there?" He pointed to a senior toddling away with his walker.

I nodded.

"I've already told him four times today. He can't remember past five minutes, so he keeps asking me to tell it again." Bart slapped his knees.

Truman took the knee slapping as an invitation to visit with Bart, who obliged and ruffled the dog's neck.

"Besides," Bart continued, "now that I have an audience, I can share all my old detective stories. If I run out of those, I'll make up something."

I put my hand on Bart's shoulder. "You were the key to making this a success."

Juan walked up and scratched Truman behind one ear.

"Can I give you a hug?" he asked.

"Sure."

His long arms enveloped me and squeezed gently.

Putting a hand on Bart's shoulder, Juan asked, "Did this fella tell you that he almost blew the whole set up?"

I shook my head.

"After you stuck your head in the room and closed the door, this clown whispered, 'Make my day.' I almost burst out laughing. The pile of blankets covering me would have looked like an earthquake."

"I think Bart is going to keep this place smiling. He's might put Truman and me out of a job," I said.

"Not on your life," Bart said. "You better come back often to visit."

"I will. I wouldn't want to miss this action packed place."

———

I pulled into my driveway anticipating a relaxing evening on the deck with Jerry. A strange car sat in front of my house. The screen door was closed, but the front door was open. I drove straight up the hill to Jeanine and Rocky's house.

Rocky answered the door. "There's someone inside my house. Did you give a key to someone?" I asked.

Rocky's eyes narrowed. "No, let me go down there with you."

I turned the car around, and through the trees, we could barely see a figure walking out on my deck.

"Looks like someone is making himself at home," Rocky said.

"I cannot imagine who."

We walked around to the back of the house.

I stopped and grabbed Rocky's arm. "Morgan! That's my son!"

"I guess you aren't in danger then."

Rocky shook hands with Morgan, "Hi, I'm Rocky. My wife Jeanine and I are the property owners here. Come on up to the house and meet her and our critter crew. By the way, how did you get in the house?"

Morgan glared at me. "Key under the mat."

"Oops," I said.

Rocky grunted, gave me a 'you know better' look, and walked back up the hill.

Morgan hugged me hard. It hurt good. "It's wonderful to see you, Mom."

My heart soared. Nothing compared to hugs and seeing his face in person.

"I had a flight change in Memphis, so I took a few days off and rented a car. I thought you could use some company."

I hugged him again as hard as I could.

"Can I take you out to a local dive for dinner?" he asked.

"Um, a friend is coming over to make dinner for me."

"Friend, is this a girl friend?"

"No." My face grew hot.

"Do you want me to make myself scarce?"

"I would have liked family introductions to be on my timing, but I surrender to circumstance. I'll text Jerry and ask him to cook for three."

We chatted on the deck until Jerry arrived and joined us.

Morgan stood. "Morgan Vonn. Nice to meet you."

"Jerry Elliston. Glad to meet you."

When their hands connected in that ancient peace greeting, something inside me warmed.

"Mom tells me you're a vet," Morgan said, his eyes twinkling.

I threatened him with my 'don't you dare' stare.

"Yes. What brings you here to your mom's?"

"It was time to visit. She seemed a bit edgy when I talked to her last. She has a hard time fibbing face to face." He grinned.

"She has been under a bit of pressure lately. I've been keeping an eye on her for you." Jerry said.

"Thank you, I appreciate that. All this murder stuff she told me about has gotten under her skin. She needs someone to check up on her," Morgan said.

"Guys, please don't talk about me like I'm not here. I can fend for myself."

"Sure, mom."

"Of course," Jerry said and cocked his head.

Jerry and Morgan nodded toward each other, grinning.

"Can we go somewhere else with this conversation, please?" I was not sure if their ganging up on me was a good or bad thing.

"I talked to Nick today," Jerry said.

"Did he have any information about Judith? I tried texting and calling all day and she never responded."

"Client privilege. He couldn't confirm anything."

I frowned.

"Can I ask you a few questions?" Morgan asked.

"Is this an interrogation?"

"Not at all."

"Then shoot."

"Did you ever consider that Judith might be in on the whole 'murder and custody' thing?"

"Are you telling me that you think Judith might be involved with the murders?"

"I didn't say that, did I? But each master plan needs a master planner," Morgan said.

"That would mean Judith and Paul knew each other before she came here. It is doubtful that two strangers would have contrived this plan," Jerry said.

Morgan nodded, "They likely did, either that or Paul fell in love with Judith at first sight and was willing to do anything for her."

"You have got to be kidding. Judith a mastermind? No way," I said.

"Morgan's right, planners are essential. She worked at the bank that serviced Meredith's loan. Maybe she caught wind of the pending will change," Jerry said.

"So, hypothetically, if Judith was involved, the police would be looking for her," I said.

"They would. But great master planners plan an escape route in case the plan goes south," Jerry said.

"You have GOT to be kidding. She is so nice."

"He's not kidding, Mom. She could have been putting it on. If she was in on it, she could have been an experienced charlatan."

Morgan's poor-mom grin rankled me. "There's nothing I can do to change the past." I was talking more to myself than them.

"Nope. Let's make dinner," Jerry said.

Morgan and I helped chop and dice and Jerry cooked a magnificent stir-fry. After we cleaned up and put away the dishes, we all went out on the deck for a green tea mochi.

"Do you know where Judith works?" Morgan asked.

"She works at a bank."

"Did you call the bank and see if Judith showed up for work?"

"I didn't think about that. I'll do it as soon as they open in the morning. Oh, I forgot, Charlotte was going to send me Judith's address.

I scrolled through my messages. "Here it is, 64 Morning Dove Lane. You men want to go for a ride?"

We piled into Jerry's Jeep and I plugged the address into my map app. Fifteen minutes later, we pulled up to an empty lot.

I jumped out of the Jeep. Jerry and Morgan followed me onto the sparse grass and weeds.

"Does Judith live under a rock?" Morgan asked.

"He definitely inherited the sarcastic gene," Jerry said.

I poked Jerry with my elbow.

"I'll text Charlotte to make sure this is right address."

Charlotte's text shot back bookended with two happy face emojis. "Yes, sweetie. She also gave a PO box where we sent mail." I showed the text to Morgan and Jerry.

"Maybe there's an underground house?"

"Morgan!"

Jerry shook his head. "I'm not sure about you two."

I walked around the lot in random circles. Who was this woman? Did she cause havoc everywhere? I kicked a rock. It hit near Morgan and bounced off something semi-solid.

Morgan bent down examining the object that bounced the rock. "By any chance, did this Judith lady have a Welsh corgi?" Morgan asked.

My heart sank. Surely, neither she nor Paul would have harmed her dog. NO! No way! As I rushed over to Morgan, he bent down and picked up a round sign. He turned the sign toward me. It was a yellow winky happy face with a corgi sticker attached across the forehead.

"Mastermind," Morgan said.

"She is ahead of us by leaps and bounds. If Judith had the foresight to establish a false address, she must have had all the details and possibilities planned out way in advance," I said.

"Slick lady. I wager you'll find she wasn't at work today," Jerry said.

"With her planning abilities, I doubt anyone will ever find her. I assume she was new in town?" Morgan asked.

I nodded. "She setup Paul. She knew about Meredith being sick and then getting better. I bet they knew each other long before they came here. It was no coincidence that she arrived at precisely the right time. I don't like Paul, but I hate to see him end up being the only one held responsible for the deaths."

"He did do the dirty work," Jerry said.

"Isn't planning murder a crime?" I asked.

"It is complicity, mom. She was an accomplice. But if it's all 'he said-she said,' and there is no hard proof, I doubt she could be convicted."

"But she ran," I said.

"She can claim she was afraid of Paul," Jerry said.

"But she gave a false address," I said.

"That's not much evidence. There could be a lot of reasons for giving this address, like this is where she was planning to build."

"It's just not fair that she skipped town," I said.

"Since when is life fair?" Morgan asked.

I bowed my head in submission to life, then headed back to the Jeep with Morgan and Jerry close behind.

No one spoke on the way home. We pulled in to my house and Truman decided we would all go for an evening stroll.

"Does that dog run your life?" Morgan asked.

"Pretty much so."

"Spoiled."

"Yep, and he's not my only spoiled child."

Morgan chuckled. "Lucky you."

Truman discovered an old ball hidden in the weeds and brought it to me.

"I'm tired. Play ball with your little brother." I tossed the ball to Morgan.

He teased Truman with the ball and headed out into the open pasture to play fetch.

"Are you okay?" Jerry asked.

"I guess." I focused on a violet poking out of the gravel near my feet.

Jerry put his hands on my shoulders. I turned my face to his. We stood searching each other's eyes. Slowly Jerry pulled me against him, sliding his arms around me in a tight hug. His chest felt secure under my cheek. He put his head against my hair and held tight.

He released his hold and cupped my chin in his hand pulling it upward until our eyes met. Leaning down he gently pressed his lips on mine. His mustache tickled.

For an instant, I froze but then melted my lips into his. It had been forever since my lips had felt the passion of a kiss. I pressed my lips harder. Jerry's hand pressed the back of my head and massaged away all the tension.

A galloping 75-pound dog sideswiping our legs knocked us apart. Truman dropped the ball at my feet and wagged his tail. Jerry picked up the ball and we turned toward the pasture so he could throw it.

Fifty feet away, Morgan's teeth gleamed in a huge smile. He waved. "Come on, Truman, bring it here," his voice singsong.

Truman flopped on the ground, panting. Together we watched the sky slide from blue to pink while Truman took a minute to cool and catch his breath. The sun reflected off the westward sides of the clouds turning them Midas gold.

The four of us continued down the gravel road. Jerry took my hand, and it was right. The only sounds were our footsteps and the diverse calls of a mockingbird, and the high-pitched chirps of evening insects.

"I forgot to tell you what else happened today," Jerry said.

"Something happy, not horrid, I hope."

"Carley and Tara dropped by today to get a checkup for their new Golden Retriever puppy."

"I'm glad Carley is starting to live a normal life. The girl deserves it."

"They asked me for your contact information. I hope you don't mind, I gave it to them."

"That's fine. Do you know what they wanted it for?"

"A couple of things. They wanted you to know that the other day Ben was sorting Meredith's effects and came across her cell phone. They charged it to get her photos and see if there were any messages they needed to address."

"And?" I asked.

"Two days before Meredith died there was a message from Paul Wentworth asking Meredith to call him. The message had been played but wasn't deleted."

"That's interesting. As far as I know, she hadn't mentioned that to Ben and Tara," I said.

"Also, that afternoon the phone log registered that Meredith had returned his call and they talked for ten minutes. That was plenty of time for Meredith to tell him that she was changing the will."

"Poor Meredith. That's so circumstantial it wouldn't have helped if we had known that earlier. Talking to someone on the phone isn't a crime, but it convinces me that Paul did know about the new will," I said.

"There's something else. Carley would like to train her dog to be a therapy dog. She said before you and Truman visited Safe Acres, she was thinking about ending her life. Your visit to Safe Acres with Truman gave her hope and a goal."

"Mom, you are something special." Morgan smiled and gave me a side hug.

Truman stuck his nose under Morgan's hand and flipped it up. Morgan ruffled the fur on the dog's neck. "You're special too, you silly dog."

Jerry cocked his head, his face warm and inviting.

I blushed and realized that Truman had taught me that accepting affection, comforts others. "I don't know if I'm special. But perhaps I'm learning to connect the dots in the right order to complete the picture."

Made in the USA
Monee, IL
02 August 2025